BACHELOR DADS
Single Doctor…Single Father!

At work they are skilled medical professionals, but at home, as soon as they walk in the door, these eligible bachelors are on full-time fatherhood duty!

These devoted dads still find room in their lives for love…

It takes very special women to win the hearts of these dedicated doctors, and a very special kind of caring to make these single fathers full-time husbands!

'I knew you'd be upset,' he said softly.

Fergus leant against the wall and pushed himself off when she entered. He held open his arms and her brain said no as her heart steered her into the comfort of his embrace. She sobbed quietly for a minute or two, to ease the strain of staying strong for the last few hours, and he just held her gently until the storm was over.

Despite her tears, she did feel better, and Ailee lifted her face to thank him. But that thought caught and died as they stared at each other. There was nothing either of them could do as a force greater than their wills drew them together for a single, healing kiss.

'No.' Ailee stepped back out of his arms and her hand came up to cover her mouth. 'You said you wouldn't.'

'I did, didn't I?' Fergus looked at her and she couldn't read the expression on his face. 'I'm sorry,' he said, and walked out of the office. She felt like crying again, for a different reason.

THE SURGEON'S SPECIAL GIFT

BY
FIONA McARTHUR

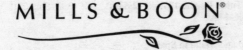

MILLS & BOON®

First published in Great Britain 2006
Harlequin Mills & Boon Limited,
Eton House, 18-24 Paradise Road, Richmond, Surrey TW9 1SR

© Fiona McArthur 2006

ISBN-13: 978 0 263 84753 6
ISBN-10:   0 263 84753 5

Set in Times Roman 10½ on 12½ pt
03-0906-44805

Printed and bound in Spain
by Litografia Rosés, S.A., Barcelona

A mother to five sons, **Fiona McArthur** is an Australian midwife who loves to write. Medical romance gives Fiona the scope to write about all the wonderful aspects of adventure, romance, medicine and midwifery that she feels so passionate about—as well as an excuse to travel! So, now that the boys are older, her husband Ian and youngest son Rory are off with Fiona to meet new people, see new places, and have wonderful adventures. Fiona's website is at www.fionamcarthur.com

Recent titles by the same author:

MIDWIFE IN NEED*
A VERY SINGLE MIDWIFE*
THE PREGNANT MIDWIFE*
DANGEROUS ASSIGNMENT *24:7*
THE DOCTOR'S SURPRISE BRIDE

Marriage and Maternity

This book was inspired by a wonderful woman,
Colleen Gilby, a live kidney donor. I dedicate
this book to Colleen, and to donors and
their families everywhere.

CHAPTER ONE

FERGUS MCVICKER noticed the woman as he waited to board his flight and a primitive and unexpected recognition slapped him in the chest as if some navigation-deficient land bird had just collided with him.

Usually he just hyperventilated as he watched the planes take off the runway.

Hell! He did not have the mental energy for lust at first sight in his crowded life. And that was apart from his irrational fear of flying. Fergus dragged his eyes away from the goddess.

'Dr Ailee Green? Would you please come to Flight Reception?' The disembodied voice of the flight-desk attendant echoed around the departure lounge.

The woman Fergus had noticed gathered her bag and coat, and stood up. Yep. She was the one. All six feet of her.

Lord, she was tall.

He'd always had a thing for women who came up to his eye level at least. His stomach clenched but this time not from the thought of the plane waiting outside the window for him to board.

Ailee Green's magnetism distracted him as she swayed calmly towards the uniformed hostess and presented her boarding pass for identification. So…she was a doctor.

She wasn't classically beautiful but something about this woman resonated with him and the way she moved made him breathless.

He shifted position so he could see the expressions on her face. Big smile, gorgeous lips and not afraid to look people in the eye and smile at them. There was something wholesome about Ailee Green that slid under the barbed-wire perimeter fence he kept locked around his heart.

The colours she'd chosen to travel in were striking among the fashionable black of the Londoners—maybe that helped. Her sleeveless emerald shirt outlined her femininity as much as the soft rusty orange trousers emphasised her height and slimness.

Dr Green made him think of Sydney on a sunny day, lunch on the pier near Luna Park, rides on the ferry across to Manly. She was a far cry from the last fortnight at St Edna's, trying to find the key to promotion of organ donation for Australia.

St Edna's had the highest rate of donation in the world and his passion was to unlock that potential at home and be able to change the lives of so many people trapped by their failed organs.

Fergus sighed and turned away. She had quietened his nerves for a few moments at least and he wondered if he'd catch a glimpse of her again. One thing about travelling first class—it was antisocial and he couldn't follow up on the crazy urge to wander over and chat her up!

The announcement to board tightened his nerves and he turned away.

When she sat down next to him for the next thirteen hours to Singapore Fergus almost forgot the plane was ready to launch itself into the sky.

Ailee Green's eyes widened as they exchanged polite glances and Fergus grimly acknowledged that she was aware of him, too. He fancied the air between them vibrated, though perhaps it was just the one hundred per cent—he had been assured—perfect engines as they prepared for take-off.

Ailee felt the heat race up her cheeks. 'Do I know you?' Her voice came out more husky than she'd intended. Damn. Her neighbour had those black eyes she'd read about but had never believed existed…and shoulders to die for. And his legs looked longer than hers. Double, triple damn.

Complications she did not need right now or for the next few months because she'd be no good for any type of liaison.

He smiled at her, black-eyed and beguiling, and Ailee melted into the seat. This guy was very practised and she steeled herself against the waves of attraction that were beating like bats against her defences.

Face it, she told herself, it was unlikely her seat companion was on the lookout for a meaningful relationship. Ailee swallowed a bubble of semi-hysterical laughter.

There was always the mile-high club—sex in the clouds—while she was well enough to do it.

Her wicked thought supported his black, bedroom eyes, and not her common sense. Ailee blushed again.

She'd never had a promiscuous episode in her life and she'd bet this guy had had plenty.

'I'm Fergus.' The gravelly tones in his voice, apparently invisibly attached to her nerve endings, raised the flesh on her arms and tightened her throat.

She licked dry lips and incredibly his eyes darkened even more. She hoped he wasn't thinking she was vamping. Lord, she was in a pickle, and she glanced around for the hostess to save her.

An angel appeared. 'Is everything all right, Dr Green?'

Ailee knew there were no free seats in the next cabin as she'd been bumped up from business class for that reason. Her hospital had paid for the other seat but would never pay her way up here in the stratosphere. There didn't look like any alternative seats here either. She'd have to stay next to this gorgeous guy and sweat it out.

'May I have an iced water, please?' Maybe that would put out the fire.

The pretty hostess smiled, as if Ailee were the most important person in the world, and then her eyes widened as she noticed Ailee's seat mate.

Tell me about it, Ailee wordlessly sympathised with the woman.

'Not fair, is it?' Ailee said softly, and the hostess met her eyes as she handed the drink across. Both women smiled in perfect understanding. Just too much a man. Yes?

At least Ailee felt she had an ally. The drink was frosty as it slid down her throat and she relaxed back in the seat and closed her eyes. She'd just pretend he wasn't there.

The engines roared. Fergus had planned to avoid conversation with the goddess but the runway was streaming past the window and this was the moment he really hated.

'Are you from Sydney?' The aircraft left the ground and his stomach clenched.

He'd broken the first-class code. Fergus never spoke to a seat mate unless eye contact gave permission, but he couldn't help himself.

Her green eyes opened and at first he thought he saw panic beneath the lashes but he must have been mistaken. Her voice was level when she spoke.

'Balmoral. In Sydney.'

She didn't ask about him but Fergus saw the clouds stream past his window, testament to how high they were off the ground already, and he told her anyway. He knew he was babbling. 'I'm from Mosman. Not that far, as the crow flies.'

'Hmm.' She smiled vaguely and closed her eyes again.

So he wasn't irresistible, Fergus mocked himself, but it was better this way. The hard part was over. The plane hadn't crashed and he could just deep-breathe himself through the rest of it until the seat-belt sign switched off.

Then she sighed and opened her eyes and he felt the warmth of her perusal.

'I'm sorry. That was rude of me.' She held out her hand and any residual flight-induced tremors quietened as he curled his grip around hers. She had thin, elegant fingers and clear nail polish that made her short nails shiny. He couldn't help a quick squeeze of her hand.

Now that he had her attention he became loath for her to lose interest. 'I don't usually harass women, but I wondered if you would mind talking just for a few more minutes.' He mocked himself. 'Embarrassing as it is, I'm terrified of flying.'

It was the last thing Ailee had expected to hear. He didn't look like he was terrified of anything. In fact, she would have bet he'd do a great stand-in for Tarzan wrestling a couple of lions.

She eased her fingers out of his death grip and looked at him properly.

Clinically.

There was a faint sheen of sweat on his upper lip and a tiny flickering tic under his left eye. She slid her fingers around his wrist. His pulse was racing. He really was nervous.

Just as the thought triggered her professional interest they hit a patch of turbulence and his face paled even more. She squeezed his wrist in sympathy and then let his arm go as he gripped the armrests.

'Sure,' she said easily. 'Flying is really not that bad, you know. I went for a spin over Edinburgh in a motorised hang glider last week and the view was breathtaking.'

He looked green at the thought and she chuckled.

He shook his head. 'Nice laugh. That makes me feel better than the story. Let's talk about something else. What's your name?'

'I'm Ailee,' she obliged, and steered the conversation away from flying. 'So, have you been to Singapore before?'

The plane dipped and righted itself. He clutched the

armrests tighter and she slid her hand across again to comfort him. She saw him breathe out consciously, like a woman in labour, and she squeezed his fingers over the side of the seat.

There was a pause until the plane settled. 'Singapore? Once. On the way over.' He spoke slowly, as if enunciation was a problem.

Poor guy. Ailee cast round in her mind for distracting conversation. She thought of the grand hotel left over from the colonial occupation of the English. 'Did you go to Raffles Hotel?'

He shook is head. 'I rarely leave my room on stopovers.'

Rain rattled against the window but she ignored it. 'You must visit. Raffles is a tradition. You should at least drop in and have a gin sling and crack some peanuts.'

'Peanuts?' His hand had loosened to just tight beneath hers.

'You'll see,' Ailee said. 'You could always go the whole way and book for high tea. Though I hear reservations take three days before you can get in.'

Then she smiled at him and Fergus felt as if he'd just opened an unexpected gift. 'You have a beautiful smile,' he said.

She smiled again and then they both just settled back without her removing her hand.

The plane levelled out and the 'Fasten Seat Belt' sign flickered and then went out. Perhaps she wouldn't notice his need had gone and still leave her hand over his. The fear had seeped away and Fergus had a feeling his phobia wouldn't be a problem again. All he'd have to do was imagine Ailee Green's hand on his and he would be at peace.

The end of that thought had a convoluted tail, like a Singapore dragon, and he shied away from it. Right now it felt as if his fingers belonged to her and he didn't want her to let them go.

When the hostess came she startled them both and Ailee quickly pulled her hand away. Fergus sighed.

'Dr Green.' The hostess was flustered. 'We have an elderly gentleman in the other cabin. He appears very unwell—can you come?'

Ailee unbuckled her seat belt immediately. 'Of course.'

Fergus admired her lack of hesitation. This was no time to reman incognito. 'If you need help, let me know. I'm a surgeon but I do know my first aid.'

Ailee, which was how he thought of her now, bestowed another slightly distracted smile and thanked him before she moved off with the flight attendant.

Fergus almost hoped she'd call him to help because he missed her company already. He pulled up his video screen and flicked through the channels.

Wonderful. Now he knew they were thirty-seven thousand feet above sea level and travelling at six hundred and fifty miles an hour. If a window blew out they would all freeze because it was minus sixty-five degrees outside.

Two minutes later the hostess was back.

'Dr Green asked if you could assist, Mr McVicker.'

When Fergus arrived he was in time to see the patient, an elderly man in tight clothes, roll his eyes back and clutch his chest.

'Cardiac arrest,' he heard Ailee mutter, and Fergus agreed silently as he knelt down and loosened the collar around the man's neck to feel for his carotid pulse.

'Pulseless,' Fergus agreed.

Right, then. This was it with a vengeance. Time for a med school refresher.

Surprisingly, considering how long it had been since he'd involved himself in an acute, non-surgical situation, he felt confident as the basic life support all came back to him.

The resuscitation went smoothly, largely because Ailee was so quietly efficient and Fergus understood her minimal instructions perfectly.

The hostess produced a resuscitation bag and oxygen cylinder while Fergus easily lifted the frail man into the galley where there was more room and privacy to work.

Ailee tilted his chin and fitted the mask over the gentleman's nose and mouth and began to inflate the man's lungs with rhythmic inflations of the bag. Fergus synchronised his chest compressions with the fall of the patient's chest to stimulate some cardiac output but there was no response from their patient.

'What about drugs and defibrillation?' Fergus said quietly.

'That's the good news.' Ailee was watching the man's chest closely, to ensure his lungs inflated as she worked, and she didn't move her head as she spoke.

'They have a defibrillator in the bolted box and emergency drugs in a sealed kit that can only be opened by a doctor. They're both on their way.'

The defibrillator arrived and after two shocks the man's heart settled into a steady if weak rhythm.

Ailee looked across at Fergus with a slight smile. 'I always wondered if defibrillation would cause the cabin lights to flicker.'

Fergus arched his brows. 'Obviously not. That probably means the navigation equipment is still working, too.'

Ailee broke open the drug box and a few minutes later they both sat back and watched the man as his breathing settled and his colour improved.

'Well done, Doctor.' Fergus spoke quietly and Ailee looked up.

She gave him a crooked grin. 'Bet that made you forget you were flying.'

'I'd already forgotten.' Their eyes met and Ailee blushed. She looked gorgeous when she did that.

'How long until landing?' Fergus tore his eyes away to look up at the senior steward.

'The captain said we'll be on the ground in fifteen minutes. We've diverted to Paris and an ambulance will meet us.'

When the plane took off again, Fergus barely noticed the ascent.

He knew he couldn't get involved with this woman because she was wonderful and genuine and there wasn't enough emotional depth left in him to offer any woman.

His daughter needed any reserves he had and he'd promised himself he'd never marry again and expose himself to that type of loss for a second time.

But Ailee was captivating.

Back in their seats, conversation during the flight was safe and noncommittal, and he steered away from the subject of work. To his delight, Ailee was an intriguing companion.

She'd travelled widely and had anecdotes from almost every continent, and she followed his lead and never once mentioned her role in medicine.

Fergus was careful to keep the topics general but he still found out that she lived with her younger brother and mother in a huge rambling house in Balmoral, drove a thirty-year-old Mercedes that used to belong to her father, and loved heavy metal rock as well as vintage country music.

Dinner came and went and they discussed how both had a parent who'd immigrated from Scotland, discussed cosmopolitan London and the sheer age of the Roman ruins in the Tower Of London, which surprisingly they'd both visited on this trip.

Other times they kept their own thoughts and he found her incredibly restful in the silences.

Eventually the cabin lights dimmed and everyone settled to rest for the few hours before breakfast, but despite the comfort of his sleeping pod Fergus found he couldn't sleep.

Ailee stirred emotions that had lain dormant since Stella had died. This was stormy weather, worse than turbulence in flight, and he needed to be careful, but would it be so dangerous to spend more time with Ailee—at least until after Singapore?

Maybe he could have twenty-four hours of a dream

in Singapore, time out from the real world with Ailee, and recharge his faith in the good times that were out there, as long as they both obeyed the rules. His mouth compressed. As long as he obeyed the rules!

The plane flew on and finally breakfast arrived as the blinds were raised. A pale sunrise pinked the sky outside the windows and a few minutes later Ailee began to stir beside him.

'Good morning, sleepyhead.' He smiled at her tousled hair. This was how she looked in the mornings—good enough to eat. The thought stoked the fire in his belly that had simmered all night and he had to look away because if he didn't he'd lean over and kiss her properly awake.

When he had himself back under control he returned her smile. When she had woken properly and smiled at him he asked her the question that he'd deliberated on all night.

'If I secure a reservation, will you share high tea at Raffles with me?'

Ailee didn't answer immediately and he forced himself not to hold his breath.

She hesitated. 'I'm in Singapore for less than a day before I fly on to Sydney.'

He shrugged. 'It's just afternoon tea. Let me see what I can do while you at least think about it. Which hotel are you staying at?'

'Singapore Dragon.' There was that tail again. He thought he detected some reluctance in divulging the information and he reminded himself that she had every right to be wary of him.

He couldn't help being delighted at her answer, though. He smiled openly at this good luck and she did that blush thing again with her cheeks that he particularly enjoyed.

'What a coincidence. I'll let you know, then.'

CHAPTER TWO

W<small>HAT</small> was she doing?

Ailee argued with herself as she dragged her overnight case past the empty luggage carousel. She'd learnt long ago it was better to pack a few interchangeable clothes and avoid the whole luggage hassle.

Fergus McVicker just wanted a fling. She been trained long ago not to talk to strangers, especially heart-tugging handsome ones, but it had been fun.

Customs cleared quickly and she spotted her name on the hire-car driver's board as she went through the automatic doors.

'Dr Green?'

'That's right.' She handed over her case and followed the little man out to his Lexus. The Singapore heat hit her in the face and she revelled in it after the cold of Britain.

She should be resting and writing up her review of her secondment for the hospital board while she was here, not gallivanting around with the hunky Mr McVicker. He had warning signs written all over him.

Ailee barely saw the glorious red and purple bougainvillea that lined the road from the airport to the city.
During their conversations she'd become glaringly
aware that Fergus had avoided any mention of Sydney,
their work, or meeting up when they got home. Maybe
that was a good thing.

If she agreed to meet him today, afternoon tea would
lead to drinks, and drinks to dinner, and dinner to
goodness knew what! She needed to remember his lack
of interest in their mutual vocation and realise there
was no 'ever after' planned for the two of them—just a
Singapore fling. Trouble was, she was way out of her
depth as an old-fashioned girl.

His invitation hinted at a stopover seduction and, of
course, she didn't want that. Or did she? Ailee couldn't
believe how tempted she was.

Fergus had such kind eyes when you looked past the
bedroom aspect. Of course, that was hard to look past
when just the lift of his hand reminded her of his
strength and agility in the plane. Even in the midst of a
crisis, a part of her had been awed when he'd carried that
man to the galley as if he were as light as a doll.

The phobia he'd admitted to only made him more intriguing because it called to the nurturing part of her that
she'd only had the opportunity to practise on her patients
or her brother.

The quandary lay in a subliminal connection between
them and she was sure he felt it, too.

The way they flawlessly meshed during the resuscitation of that poor man.

The way she only had to half explain places she'd

visited, and he'd never seen, and yet he'd understood what she'd described perfectly.

The way they could sit in silence and feel no need to fill the gaps and—she had to admit most of all—what the touch of his fingers had done to her senses!

Imagine if he touched more than her hand! She shivered and the driver caught her eye in the mirror.

'Air-conditioner too cold, Doctor?'

Ailee felt the warmth in her cheeks. Damn. Just thinking about Fergus had her blushing, and swearing, more than she had since her teens. 'No, thank you. I'm fine.'

She stared out the window at even more building construction as they came closer to the city. So what was she going to do?

The sensible thing would be to tell Fergus she had a review to write and stay safe in her room.

The risk was she would miss out on the most incredible time of her life. Of course, then he'd probably disappear at Sydney airport and she'd spend the rest of her days searching for someone to match him!

Her inner voice of caution suggested this was not a brilliant scenario.

But what if this was her one time to cross this man's path? What if this was the real thing and she'd been too timid to risk exploring the possibility?

Damn again. If he was her perfect match, his timing was atrocious.

The next three months weren't going to be much fun for her, although she didn't for one second regret her coming operation. She just wished she'd met Fergus at a different time in her life.

Check-in at the hotel was a blur as she wrestled with her dilemma. Clarity came as the plastic key was encased in its embossed cardboard folder. She was a fool.

'Can I leave a message for another guest, please?'

Ten minutes later the force of the water on her shoulders felt wonderful after the gentle spray of the showers she had experienced in Britain, and she could feel herself relax. This was more sensible. She'd decided not to meet Fergus, and she could finish her report. She flipped open her case and slipped into her pyjamas.

The trouble was now she was unsettled as the clock digits changed and the morning traffic increased outside her window.

The doorbell rang and she quietened the flutter of panic the sound ignited. 'This is too good a hotel to give him my room number,' she said out loud to calm the thudding in her chest as she moved towards the door.

The bellboy held up an exquisite basket of delicate Singapore orchids. A note nestled among the perfect blooms.

'Dr Green?' The boy checked.

'Yes, that's me.' She took the basket from him and sighed. She resisted the urge to tip as hotels in Singapore discouraged tipping. 'Thank you.'

The boy beamed and turned away. Ailee closed the door and carried the basket across to the table under the window.

'Thank you for your hand and your delightful com-

pany on the flight from London. My room number is
2001. High tea is at three, I'll be there anyway. F'

This hotel stood only twenty stories high, which
meant he was in the penthouse. Typical. He had been in
first class after all. The flowers were beautiful and it was
only ten o'clock in the morning.

Ailee dialled his number and he picked it up on the
first ring.

'The flowers are lovely, thank you.'

'I'm glad you like them, Ailee. I wasn't trying to
change your mind.'

'Sure you were,' she drawled, and she heard him
chuckle. 'Lucky for you I need to get out. Would you
like me to show you Singapore?'

'Yes, please.'

She smiled into the phone at his simple answer.

When she met him downstairs she felt the warmth
of his appraisal and she was glad she'd agreed to
come. Heads turned as they walked across the foyer
and Ailee felt a little like a groupie accompanying a
rock star. He held her arm and showed her to the limousine he'd hired.

They rode across to Sentosa on the skyway and she
didn't notice his slight hesitation when she suggested it.

He didn't complain when she recommended they
take the elevator to the top of the giant stone lion's head
or, as they called it, the Merlion.

From the platform Ailee gazed out over the lush
greenery and away to the water and across the bay to
point out landmarks. They discussed the British influence
on Singapore and the fabulous growth of the new city.

Fergus, with laughter in his eyes, bought her a snowball with a miniature skyway as a memento.

On the way back they stopped at the Skyroom, which lay between the two ends of the aerial road over the lush greenery. They drank champagne on the edge of the open-air restaurant overlooking the unbroken view so high above the tropical gardens below.

Ailee felt as if she were flying again and not all of it was to do with their height from the ground.

She clapped her hand to her head. 'I can't believe I did this. I've taken you to so many high places and for-gotten your fear of heights.'

'I wondered when you'd remember that.' Fergus shook his head and relaxed back into the lounge, thinking how beautiful she was. 'That's why I bought you the snowball. As a thank-you.'

Ailee looked incredible, Fergus thought, as she leaned against the red cushions in her Singapore-red sundress with her long legs bent at the knee and casually crossed at the ankle. He struggled to keep the conver-sation going as his libido rose.

What were they discussing? That's right—his aver-sion to heights.

'It's the actual plane, not heights, I don't like. I'm afraid the whole motorised flight concept makes me shudder. The cable car isn't my favourite vehicle either but...' his glance brushed over her and he smiled '...strangely, I'm much calmer about it now.'

She leant towards him as if he was the most fascinat-ing person in the world and the cynical side of Fergus dreaded her finding out he was just a shell.

But he didn't feel a shell when he was with her. He felt buoyed up by her energy, intoxicated by her laugh, alive for the first time in two years, and the first thoughts of following the acquaintance up in Sydney crept past his caution.

The waiter arrived with their seafood lunch and the conversation moved away from the personal as they discussed their plans for the rest of the day.

Their driver suggested a route to the rainforest and the promise of tranquillity attracted them. Once surrounded by the serenity of the trees and lush greenery they both heaved a sigh of relief to escape the crowds.

As they walked a leafy trail to a waterfall Fergus held Ailee's hand in his and even managed to comment sensibly on native birds and several dragon lizards, despite the fact that all he could think of was the feel of her skin against his.

They discussed environmental issues and wildlife protection, and by the time they were back in the city they were ready for afternoon tea at the magnificent white-columned Raffles under the rows of waving ceiling fans.

They started in Raffles famous bar and Ailee dragged him by the hand to a table between the magnificent staircase and the window overlooking the terrace. Tropical birds chattered outside the window and tourists laughed and cracked nuts as they sipped their umbrella'd drinks.

A bowl of peanuts, still in their shells, sat in the middle of the table and Fergus glanced down as his feet crunched over the discarded shells that covered the floor.

He raised his eyebrows at Ailee and she laughed.

'It's all part of the atmosphere,' she said.

A pretty waitress carried her order book over to their table. 'Gin slings?' she asked, branding them as tourists.

'Yes, please,' Ailee answered before Fergus could say anything, and as she turned to him and smiled he would have drunk dishwater if she'd asked at that moment.

'You have to drink a gin sling when you come here, it's part of the tradition.'

He cracked a nut and offered her the bean-shaped centre. 'And eat peanuts?'

'Absolutely.' She took the nut and lifted the shells from his palm to discard them wickedly on the floor, as others were doing.

'More customs?' he said lazily, and savoured the way she slid the nuts into her mouth. He closed his eyes and struggled to divert his thoughts. 'So you've been here before?' Inane, but at least he'd said something.

Ailee looked around and he enjoyed the pleasure on her face. 'I love it. The bar used to be much longer but I still adore the fans that are all joined together across the ceiling.'

His question came out sooner than he'd intended. 'So what are your plans when you get home?'

She looked away from him and disappointment clouded his euphoria. That wasn't a good sign.

'I'm tied up for a few months with a family thing so I'm off work until that's finalised,' she said.

Fergus tried to regain some of the closeness he could feel slipping away. Maybe she was homesick. 'Families are important, even when things aren't so smooth on the home front. I'm not a great parent, I'm afraid. There's just myself and my daughter.'

Ailee opened her mouth to ask a question but the moment was postponed as the waitress arrived with their drinks.

Why was he telling her this? He needed to shut up before he drove her away. He lifted his glass and his first sip was cautious. Thankfully the drink wasn't as bad as he'd feared it would be.

Ailee watched him and he tried to keep his face noncommittal. 'You thought you'd hate it, didn't you?' she accused him teasingly.

Fergus took another sip. 'I'm not a gin fan but this is very pleasant.'

'You can only have one because they are very expensive and I'm paying.' Ailee reached out and stole the bill before he could look.

That made him smile. 'Who said you were paying?'

'I did.' Ailee raised her chin. 'If I pay now I don't have to feel bad about you paying for lunch and afternoon tea.'

'It's a deal.' He held out his hand and she hesitated before she put her hand in his. Their eyes met and he remembered the sensation as soon as they touched. He had the feeling she did, too.

They sat there for a moment and then Ailee eased her fingers out of his hold and picked up her glass. She stared out the window and swallowed her cocktail as if it were medicine. 'I think we'd better go for afternoon tea. They have a strict timetable.'

Now what was going on in her head? Fergus finished

his own drink and stood to pull out her chair. He watched her leave Singapore dollars on the bill and smile at the waitress as the girl approached. 'Thank you, that was lovely,' Ailee said.

'You are welcome.' The girl smiled and Fergus liked it that Ailee had made the effort. A lot of the women he knew wouldn't have bothered to show their appreciation and he stored that away as another reason to follow this woman up.

When they were seated in the more formal room for afternoon tea Ailee looked more at ease and he relaxed back into the chair. 'I've really enjoyed the day with you, Ailee. Thank you for your company.'

Ailee grinned. 'Wait until you taste the cakes.'

Fergus looked across where another couple were choosing from the cart. 'My daughter is the cake lover, not me.'

'You didn't think you'd like the gin sling.' She put her elbows on the table and rested her chin on her hands to watch him. 'Will you tell me about your daughter?'

Fergus gazed out the window into the branches of the tree that brushed the side of the building, and in his mind's eye he saw his daughter. She was glowering at him. 'Sophie is twelve and very clever. Since her mother died we haven't had much common ground.' He hadn't meant to say the last sentence but that's what happened when you started to let people in. Conversation became a landslide.

Ailee's eyes widened and she looked away. Well, he'd blown that by being honest. He didn't want her to think he didn't care about Sophie. 'I've tried to be there for her but it hasn't worked that well. My wife died just before Sophie turned ten and it's been hard to talk to my daughter since then.'

Her gaze returned to his and he realized he'd been mistaken. She wasn't distancing herself, just giving him time to organise his thoughts.

'So, since then you've brought your daughter up on your own?' she asked.

'My housekeeper and her husband are surrogate grandparents.' Fergus knew how lucky he'd been. 'I don't know what I would have done without them.'

She stirred her tea. 'Why do you feel that you don't get on with your daughter?' Ailee chewed her lip and he appreciated she was wary of crossing boundaries.

A few women he knew weren't worried about boundaries and he'd never talked to anyone about Sophie before. Maybe he should have. A woman's perspective might help.

He hated the lost closeness with his daughter but despaired he'd ever regain that rapport.

'My wife, Stella, died after a routine operation. The shock of her mother's death destroyed Sophie's ability to trust me or my profession. After all, I'd said, "Mummy will be fine."'

He shook his head at the waste. 'We all assumed it would be a simple operation and convalescence. The operation was minor but the consequences a disaster. She formed a clot post-operatively and died of a pulmonary embolus.'

'I'm sorry.' Ailee sipped and then put her teacup back in the saucer. He liked the way she took her time before rushing into gushes of sympathy. 'It would be terrible for a young girl to lose her mother at that age. It must be doubly hard for you.'

He didn't want her pity, just a suggestion to help with his daughter maybe. Or perhaps he should never have started this conversation. 'Sophie is in high school. I was doing such a poor job of keeping her happy I've enrolled her at a boarding school through the week until we sort it out.'

Her eyebrows went up. 'Does she like that?' Ailee sounded doubtful that any child would be impressed with that idea.

He thought about his answer. 'It's early days but Sophie is self-sufficient and likes company.'

'Or is good at pretending,' Ailee muttered.

He sighed. 'She can't be worse off than she was with me. We fought about everything.'

Ailee seemed determined to disapprove of Sophie in boarding school but she had no idea how hard it had been. The last time Sophie had run from the room crying he'd vowed he'd have to find a way to make her happier.

Fergus tried to see where she disagreed. 'I thought boarding school with other girls might help.'

Her look said she had reservations that boarding school was the answer. 'It's none of my business. It would probably work well for you if you work long hours.'

Relieved, Fergus nodded and ignored the way Ailee's comment had pricked his confidence about Sophie's schooling. He'd save those thoughts for later review.

They both stirred their tea. Fergus broke the silence. 'Tell me about your childhood.'

She smiled. 'I get boring.'

'Feel free to bore me.' He didn't think he would ever tire of listening to her voice.

Ailee shrugged and her gaze drifted around the room. 'My dad was a fun guy and we did lots of mad things. He had his pilot's licence and an old rag and tube aeroplane that was so noisy you had to wear earmuffs to protect your ears.'

'Where did he keep an aeroplane in the city?'

Ailee smiled at the memories. 'At the aerodrome near Camden, but it's a lot busier now than it was when I was a child. We'd drive down on Sundays and have a picnic and fly a few circuits and he'd let me steer through the clouds.'

He could imagine a little girl like Ailee bouncing up and down on a seat as they'd driven to the outlying airport to have fun with her dad. He wished he had memories like that with Sophie. Maybe he needed to make some happen—just not with a plane. 'It sounds great, except for the flying part.'

Ailee looked up at the humour in his voice and she grinned at him. 'But I like aeroplanes and you don't.'

'Did you do anything on the ground that was fun?'

She nodded and her eyes sparkled. 'Dad had a passion for boats for a while and we tried sailing.'

'Now, I can enjoy a day sailing.' Fergus was enjoying the way her face lit up at her memories.

Ailee shook her head. 'We had to sell the boat because if the sea rolled we all got seasick and there was no one left to steer while we fell around the deck, throwing up over the side.'

'Well, thanks for the graphic detail,' Fergus teased.

'No problem.' She sat back and her eyes crinkled, and he realised how fortunate he was to be here at this minute with this woman opposite him.

'This is a great room.' Fergus tried to hide the sudden swirls of desire that were hitting him like the waves Ailee had just talked about.

Unfortunately, the colonial surroundings didn't prove as distracting as Fergus had hoped, but, then, he didn't think any location would drown out what he wanted to do.

'Isn't it?' Ailee glanced around and then sighed back into the chair. 'I love this place.'

Fergus needed to hold Ailee close in his arms, and maybe run his fingers down her amazing cheekbones and circle her beautiful mouth with his fingertip, before doing what he needed to do—kiss her.

'I said, aren't you going to have any food?' Ailee was smiling at him and he blinked and came back to the present.

The waiter stood resplendent in his uniform beside their table. Importantly, the man presided over a silver-handled trolley festooned with tiny delicate cakes and slices, and waited for a decision.

Fergus wasn't that kind of hungry.

'I think you need your bed,' Ailee said as she accepted a miniature butterfly cake onto her plate.

'I think I do, too.' His voice came out softer and deeper than he'd intended and there was no doubt what he meant. He watched the blush run up her cheeks.

Fergus cleared his throat. 'I'm sorry. I must be tired. I've gone absent-minded on you.' He chose a chocolate slice he didn't want and forced himself to swallow past his dry throat.

This woman had him in a state he hadn't been in since he'd been a raw youth. It was almost amusing.

'Perhaps we could meet for dinner after we've both had a few hours' sleep,' Fergus suggested.

'I'd like that,' she said.

Half an hour later the trip back to their hotel was accomplished in silence but the tension simmered between them even after the limousine door was opened by the doorman.

Things had changed since afternoon tea. Ailee had felt it at the table. The ease she'd felt with Fergus was now overlaid with an awareness that both of them were trying to hide.

Maybe it had been the discussion of families or maybe it had just grown during the time they'd spent together. Ailee wasn't sure but there was no denying they were very aware of each other.

When Fergus cupped her elbow as they stood together and waited for the lift, Ailee felt the warmth of his hand as if she'd brought a bubble of the Singapore heat from outside into the air-conditioned coolness of the hotel.

The lift bell sang its chime and the golden doors opened in front of them. Fergus stretched one hand out and raised his eyebrows questioningly.

'Ten,' Ailee said softly, and he pressed her floor button along with his own. Half of her sighed with relief and the other chewed her lip with indecision.

If she said something she knew he would come to her

room, but she couldn't do it. She didn't know him that well. They had met barely twenty-four hours ago. So why did she feel she knew this man on a level she'd never known any man?

Fergus squeezed her elbow and slid his hand down her arm as he turned her to face him. She felt the heat slice through her.

'Thank you for your company,' he said as the lift stopped at her floor and he leaned across to kiss her.

The moment his lips touched hers, the restraint they'd both held seemed to disappear into thin air. All thoughts of leaving the lift were lost and she stepped closer. Then his arms came around her and all the dancing around the attraction that flared between them was a waste of precious time, because this was where she wanted to be.

Fergus's hip pressed into hers and there was no doubt the feeling was fiercely mutual.

The automatic doors chimed as they closed on the tenth floor and the lift carried them swiftly to the top floor of the building.

Ailee didn't know how they passed through the penthouse door but obviously Fergus had found his key and inserted the card successfully, because when she opened her eyes she was being carried across the room in his strong arms.

Ailee sank her head back against his gorgeous chest. She'd always had a weakness for muscular chests. No one had actually carried her for many years—not since she'd grazed her knees as a skinny five-year-old—and Fergus carried her as if she were still as tiny as a child.

She savoured being whisked through the rooms in

this man's arms and she could almost believe she was one of those petite women she'd always admired.

He settled her at the edge of his bed and traced her brow with his finger as if she were the most fragile of Dresden china.

'You captured me the first time I saw you. Do you know that?' His quiet words lifted the hairs on her arms and she smiled at the way this man could make her feel more sensations and emotions than any man from her past.

Her mouth was dry again from nerves. 'When I sat next to you on the plane?' She remembered that moment. She'd thought she'd been the only one who'd been aware of attraction.

He traced her cheeks and lips and pressed a soft, fleeting kiss on her mouth before going on. 'Before that. In the terminal, across a crowded room, like in all the best movies, you shone like a star.'

There was nothing she could do against the power he held over her. He was kind and funny and the sweeping conversations they'd had exposed the ferocity of his intellect. She felt as if she'd found someone who understood her.

When he drew her into his arms there was no real world, only Fergus to be lost in.

He kissed her again and she was swept into a storm of sensation as the taste and feel of him surrounded her.

His strength and gentleness created havoc as he slipped her dress straps down her arms and exposed her body to the air-conditioned coolness in the room.

Her fingers flew as she unbuttoned his shirt and

slipped her hands beneath the fabric to run them over the hard planes of his chest. She needed to feel his skin under her hands and against her own skin.

She felt tiny and captured and fiercely desired by this golden man above her, and she reached up and stroked his strong neck and shoulders as he lowered his face to kiss her.

There was nothing she could do against the power he held over her. The rights and wrongs of this craziness, her fading nervousness and knowing she couldn't follow up their encounter in Sydney were all swept aside as her body responded to the feel of him against her.

The shrill sound of the room telephone finally penetrated the fog that surrounded them both.

CHAPTER THREE

FERGUS groaned and reached with one hand to lift the phone. With the other he reached for Ailee's fingers to stop her distancing herself from him. But his caller did that.

'Sophie! How are you? What do you mean, not good?' Fergus let go of Ailee's hand and turned his shoulder to face away from her. His voice dropped in volume and Ailee looked away.

What was she doing here? She pulled the top of her dress up and slid to the edge of the bed.

Sophie had already lost her mother and she didn't need her father worrying about another woman. Let alone one who was going into surgery for an operation that was anything but minor.

Maybe she could search him out when all this was over, if she was well and had something to offer him.

If he was interested. She looked around the room and reluctantly thanked Fergus's daughter for the phone call.

Ailee's loyalties lay in a different direction for the next few months and she couldn't divide herself at this point.

He put the phone down and gave her a whimsical smile. 'Where were we?'

'I was about to leave.'

'Because my daughter rang?' he said.

'Because this isn't the right time for this.'

Fergus raised his eyebrows. 'What else have you got planned that makes this timing so bad?'

She nearly told him then but what if he said that didn't matter when she knew it did? What if he tried to talk her out of the operation—not that he could—but it would create more dilemmas that she couldn't face. Better to leave the whole subject alone.

She said, 'It's a family thing.'

His face twisted into a cynical smile. 'What if this is our one chance?'

She lifted her eyes to his and acknowledged that the concept was possible but there was nothing she could do about that. Look where it had got her. Sitting on a bed with a stranger. 'That would be sad but I can't do this now.'

'I think it would be more like a tragedy. This could be the start of something special, Ailee. Do you feel that?'

She nodded but her heart told her she really should go.

'Let's slow the whole thing down. We could do something really radical like sleep together without sex. Platonic but companionable. Come and lie back down beside me. We could both rest, even sleep. I've been awake all night, and when we wake up you could have dinner with me.'

He patted the bed. 'I'll put my shirt back on. Just lie beside me and we can talk.' Fergus smiled at her and any resistance she'd had melted like snow in Singapore. 'And I could hold your hand.'

If any other man had promised her bed with no seduction she would have doubted his assurance. But somehow when Fergus said it she could believe him. If she didn't make love with him, then she hadn't lied and hadn't led him on too much, and she wouldn't burn in hell. It was so darned attractive an idea.

'I won't sleep.' She dithered.

'Then just rest.' He patted the bed again. 'We'll eat here later if we feel like it so we don't have to get changed. It's much more fun here than in your lonely room.'

That was true and the bed was soft and the cushions indulgent feather. His hand slid into hers and she lay back down beside him. He didn't try anything, and his hand held hers warmly but not with too much pressure. Slowly she relaxed. After some desultory conversation, to her surprise, her eyes grew heavy.

When Ailee woke up she was less sure she was doing the right thing by Fergus.

The room was dark and Fergus breathed deeply beside her. She gazed at the ceiling and thought of what lay ahead of her. She hadn't forgotten, just been submerged under the powerful forces of the man lying asleep beside her.

Ailee contemplated her impending operation and the undeniable risks attached to only having one kidney, not huge risks statistically but risks nevertheless.

There were physical restrictions for the first few months and changes in body image she would have to come to terms with, like a scar and tenderness.

Her brother's ill health had to be considered and her commitment to stay on standby until the timing was medically perfect for him to be a recipient.

Then Fergus had mentioned how difficult his relationship with his daughter had become, let alone the risk of bringing back all Sophie's memories of her mother's death after surgery.

Ailee couldn't do it to them and in reality he wouldn't want her to. No matter how much she could dream at this moment—she knew she would have reservations later on, and so would he. Fergus would probably have reservations as soon as he woke up.

The words he'd spoken had fitted so well with what had gone between them and what she'd most wanted to hear but in the cold light of day she couldn't allow herself to listen to him or acknowledge his power over her.

It was better to stop now and see what the future held, if anything, when her family commitments had been met.

Ailee looked across at the sleeping man, his face gentle in repose.

She couldn't tell her family about Fergus either.

Her mother and brother would say that they couldn't risk her early relationship with Fergus and call off the whole thing again.

It had taken her so long to get through to her family that she didn't consider donating her kidney a sacrifice. It was a privilege to be able to so vastly improve her brother's quality of life at such little personal cost.

'Fergus, I'm sorry,' she whispered, and swallowed the tears in her throat.

Ailee rose, dressed and scribbled briefly on the

embossed hotel notepad beside the bed. Shivering, she let herself out.

It felt surreal to come from a stranger's hotel room, dressed in her day clothes, her lips still swollen from his kisses and the scent of him still on her clothes. How could this have happened?

After a scalding shower that didn't warm her, Ailee lay and stared at the ceiling. She half expected him to ring her or knock at her door. She wasn't hungry.

She booked her reminder call for the flight and fell asleep, waiting. She told herself she'd known he hadn't meant that he wanted to see her again.

It was six a.m. and Sydney airport wasn't crowded when Ailee's flight docked at Terminal One.

With no heavy luggage, Ailee passed quickly through customs and she came out into the arrivals hall to see her mother waiting for her.

Helen Green looked like a slightly older version of her daughter and Ailee hugged her mother for comfort and was hugged strongly back.

It was so good to see her.

'Where's William?'

Her mother met her concerned look with one of her own. 'In hospital, I'll tell you in the car.'

Ailee's heart sank even further. 'Let's get out of here, then.' She didn't want to look around to see if anyone was meeting Fergus.

Helen paused and turned to study her daughter searchingly. 'Are you OK?'

'Fine.' Ailee glanced down at her luggage. 'Just

tired.' She didn't want to see the concerned look from her mother. 'William would have enjoyed the bustle of the airport,' she said to divert attention away from herself. She remembered the souvenirs, different coloured singing bagpipes that would drive her mother mad, and smiled.

'Come on, Mum. I need a cup of your tea and I've presents to distribute.'

When Fergus heard the click of the door his hand slid across and found the warmth of the sheets next to him instead of the warmth of Ailee's body. He shuddered at the sense of loss that swept over him.

'Ailee?' He looked towards the bathroom but the door was open and there were no sounds in the penthouse. She'd gone. Just like that. After the day they'd shared. As if it were nothing. He shook his head, unable to believe she'd slipped away without telling him.

He hadn't picked that in her but maybe he'd pushed too fast.

He still couldn't believe she'd gone until he sat on the edge of the bed and his glance fell on the note she'd written.

'Thank you for the day. Ailee.' That was it. Nothing else.

At least she hadn't left him money. He feared she'd pierced the shell he'd sworn to keep intact—and he wasn't sure the wound would heal at all well.

Obviously she'd not been mutually affected. So much for her agreement they should meet in Sydney. He remembered the way she'd first ignored him in the plane and he wished, bitterly, that she hadn't turned to him a few minutes later. How could such a short encounter affect him so much?

When he landed at Sydney airport Fergus handed the trolley over to his driver and scanned the arrivals hall until he caught a glimpse of Ailee as she left with another woman.

Disappointment made him catch his breath. Apart from a glimpse of her up ahead when they'd boarded at Singapore, Fergus hadn't seen Ailee since before she'd left his room the evening before.

Ailee had travelled the last leg in business class and he guessed that was lucky because if he'd had to sit and watch her for the flight to Sydney he would have weakened and suggested they meet at least one more time. He hated weakness—especially in himself.

Fergus sighed and followed his driver. It was better to suffer a little now because if watching her leave was this bad after an international flight and a day in Singapore then long-term exposure to the woman could be fatal.

A sudden uneasy thought made him wonder if there was another reason she hadn't stayed, that she was ill, awaiting medical results—heaven forbid, terminal—but then he shook his head. He'd never seen anyone healthier or more physically fit than the woman he had lain beside last night. His groin clenched and he gritted his teeth.

It was incredible that their time together hadn't been as special for her as it had been for him. Maybe he was too much of a gentleman for her. Maybe he should have pushed his advantage when he'd had it, but he'd seen something more precious than a one-night stand in Ailee. Obviously he'd been mistaken.

He lacked practice since Stella had died but he'd have sworn he'd touched Ailee during their time together. He was a fool and a besotted one at that. No wonder he'd shied away from new relationships—obviously times had changed.

He and Sophie made a good team. He might check with his daughter again to find out if the boarding-school thing was working though.

In her mother's car, Ailee cast one final look towards the terminal and then she faced the front.

'So how is William?'

Her mother's voice was heavy with concern. 'He's had a bad week. His creatine level is sky high and his electrolytes are all over the place.'

Ailee knew the strain this worry put on her mother.

Helen went on. 'He's so weak he can only take two hours of dialysis for the next few days. Hopefully he'll be able to build up his tolerance and extend the length to gain strength for the operation.'

Ailee pressed her hand on her mother's shoulder in comfort.

'He'll pull through, Mum. He's a fighter.'

'It's been so terrible, watching him. He's so young for this.' Ailee could hear the tremor in her mother's voice as she listened.

Ailee needed to hear. 'Tell me.'

'The convulsions and the body rash have been the worst but he's so tired and nauseous. I think they'll decide on your transplant in the next few weeks if he can get well enough to undergo the operation.'

'That's a good thing.' Ailee's voice was firm with conviction. She wanted to do this and see her brother well and her mother's greatest fears put aside.

'I can't wait for it all to be over and William to get his life back. To see energy and colour in his face will be worth everything. He's eighteen, for heaven's sake. He should be out chasing girls.'

As she said it a sudden vision of Fergus's face above hers made her wince, and she was glad that her mother was driving and couldn't hear her tiny sigh for what might have been, but the thought was fleeting. William was the important one.

That night Helen came to Ailee's room. 'I'm still not convinced you should do this, darling.'

Ailee hugged her and sat her down on the bed beside her. 'Look, Mum, the only drawback I can see is no contact sport, and I was never that good at netball anyway.' She tried to lighten her mother's concerns.

She ticked another concern off on her fingers. 'I will always have to wear a seat belt in the car in case of accidents but I would have anyway. Diet and exercise are not something I have a problem with, except for the occasional chocolate biscuit.'

Both women smiled because Ailee's weakness for chocolate-covered biscuits was a joke in the family.

Helen chewed her lip. 'What about childbearing? When you get married?'

'If I get married! I'm nearly thirty and no knight on a charger has chatted me up yet.' She looked away.

Now, that was the first lie she'd ever told her mother!

Helen missed her daughter's lack of conviction. 'But he's out there somewhere. With one kidney there is some increase of risk if you became pregnant.'

'Mother.' Ailee grasped Helen gently by the shoulders and looked into her worried eyes. 'We both want William well. Some people are born with one kidney and never have a moment's problem. I could get hit by a bus tomorrow and lose a kidney or worse. Even someone who's had a kidney transplant can have a baby. We've been all through this and I'm sure this is what I want.'

Helen couldn't hide the relief that warred with her worry. 'I'm so proud of you, Ailee.'

'Fiddle.' Ailee thought little of that. 'If the roles were reversed, William would do the same for me like a shot. Stop worrying about it and let's concentrate on getting William well enough to undergo the transplant so we can all finally relax.'

CHAPTER FOUR

A WEEK later Ailee looked round her temporary co-ordinator's office at Sydney West, one of the two major transplant hospitals in New South Wales, and then settled into the worn black swivel chair.

Transplant co-ordinators didn't have much down time and when the transitory vacancy had been difficult to fill, Ailee had offered to fill the gap until the replacement sister arrived in two weeks.

Ailee was way over-qualified but the experience would stand her in good stead when she gained her consultancy.

She believed so passionately in the donor programme she could only benefit from access to another facet of the process and anticipated the day when she saw her brother William energetic and happy. That day wasn't far away.

As temporary transplant co-ordinator, Ailee would not only be responsible for the care and preparation of the computer-chosen patients needing organ donation but also for the liaison with the families of donors who had died and, of course, with live donors themselves.

She would be the one who interacted with their relatives in regard to any organ donation and the arrangement of the organ-donation procedure. Afterwards she would follow the families up and inform them of the progress of any of the recipients who had benefited from their relative's generous act.

While incumbent she hoped to help raise the profile of people signing organ-donation cards.

For the moment she needed to grab the patient list and head over to the kidney transplant unit for the morning's ward round.

As well as the head of department, Dr Lewis Harry, she knew most of the team of surgeons, physicians, nurses, pharmacists and dieticians who kept the recipients in optimum health.

As Ailee entered the airy ward there was a vibrancy about the unit that made her pause so that she had a moment to study the group of professionals up ahead before they saw her. It was the tallest man who riveted her attention and caused the heat in her face.

The last week had felt like a lifetime since she'd seen him, but one lingering look at Fergus McVicker brought back Singapore so poignantly her body shuddered as if he'd touched her again.

What was he doing here?

It hadn't been as easy as she'd hoped to go on and not think about Fergus, and he'd shared her dreams every night in her lonely bed.

Now the real man confronted her and this was the last thing she needed on the first day of her new post.

Ailee searched the rest of the team, all known to her

from her visits here with William, but delightful Dr Harry was missing.

The consultant who had recruited her for the job, and would care for both William and her, had promised to be here for her first morning.

There wasn't time to dwell on this shock because Fergus had looked up and was staring across at her. There was no mercy in his look. He didn't look surprised, so at least one of them had known in advance about this meeting.

Ailee lifted her chin and crossed the room. 'Good morning, everyone. For those who aren't aware, I'm the temporary transplant co-ordinator while Maureen's broken arm is mending and the replacement sister can start.'

Ailee ignored the icy gaze fixed on her by Fergus as her colleagues murmured their congratulations. Fergus finally looked away and Ailee breathed a tiny sigh of relief. She would have to deal with him later, though she had no idea how, as he'd obviously taken her flight without telling him in the worst possible way.

Hopefully she would be more prepared when the time for discussion came.

'Now that Dr Green has arrived, we'll get on with the round, shall we?' There was no hesitation at the end of the sentence and Fergus set off and his entourage followed.

The tiny note of censure in his comment made Ailee lift her brows in surprise but she shrugged it off. She'd been on time.

Maurice, the new young pharmacist, walked beside Ailee and she quietly asked the question uppermost in her mind.

'Where's Dr Harry?'

'His wife had a stroke last night, and Mr McVicker has been seconded from Sydney West to cover for the next few weeks. We're very lucky as he's a leader in the field and just back from Britain, like you.'

That kind of luck she could do without. 'Poor Mrs Harry.' Inwardly Ailee sighed. She seemed destined to come up against this man in her life at a time that wasn't at all convenient.

'Are you with us, Dr Green?'

This time the question was pointed and beside her she could feel the surprise emanating from Maurice. The young pharmacist raised his eyebrows at her in query. Ailee's usually placid temper began a slow burn. McVicker didn't need to make such an obvious point of his problem with her.

'Of course, Mr McVicker,' she said calmly, at least on the surface.

Ailee knew the patients they would see today because she'd come in yesterday to read all the notes and introduce herself to them. She'd ignore the consultant and concentrate on the important people in the room.

The young woman in the first bed, Jody Withers, was unable to hide her excitement.

Today was Jody's discharge day and she'd spent the last two weeks smiling since she'd woken up with her new kidney and pancreas. Jody had been on the waiting list for two years and the double-transplant call had come the day before her twenty-first birthday. She represented a bright star in a sometimes tragic area.

Jody could now forgo the thrice-weekly dialysis for her renal failure, which she'd fitted in after work, and her newly donated pancreas meant she was no longer an insulin-dependent diabetic.

The four insulin needles a day she'd lived with since she'd been ten were now a thing of the past.

'So how do you feel, Jody?' It seemed Fergus had also done his homework because Jody was quite at ease with the great man.

'Still blown away that somebody somewhere changed my life by doing this, Mr McVicker.' She closed her eyes briefly and shrugged, her young face suddenly troubled. 'I can't stop thinking about my donor's family giving permission while they dealt with losing someone they loved.'

Ailee empathised with the young woman. This was part of her job. 'Your dilemma seems to be the thought uppermost in all recipients' minds, Jody. Other recipients have said a letter to the donor family sometimes helps. You could write down your feelings and when you're happy with how it sounds we can forward your letter to your donor's family. I really believe it helps them as well to hear how much of a miracle their loved one has made possible.'

Jody's smile was strained. 'That would be wonderful, Ailee. I'll try that and bring it back when I come in for my check-up next week.'

Ailee sensed Fergus's attention on her again and she forced herself to ignore the sensations that fluttered over her skin, acknowledging it was going to be incredibly difficult to work with this man. She'd just have to keep her distance and ignore the way his presence affected her.

Fergus seemed to be managing more easily than she was but he'd had prior warning and it was different for men. She'd probably been a pleasant interlude for him.

His thoughts were where hers should be—on the patient. 'All your pathology results look perfect today, Jody.' Fergus said. 'Are you happy with your medications?'

Jody nodded. 'I have a system for taking them. Maurice has helped me work out a schedule so I feel less sick, and won't forget any of the doses. I just don't want to get fat.'

Fergus smiled at the girl. 'Some side-effects we can help a little with and Louise, the dietician, is here for you any time you need her.

'You must contact us if you become unwell or you notice change or decrease in your urine output. Try the ward phone number and if what they suggest doesn't work, this is my card. While Dr Harry is away, you can ring me on my mobile any time if you're worried.'

He passed over a small white card and Ailee was glad to see the relief on Jody's face. It was generous of Fergus to make the gesture.

The round went on.

In the next room, a young couple were scheduled for surgery the next day.

Peter was donating one of his kidneys to Emma, his wife.

Emma, blonde-haired and blue-eyed, had become extremely ill with pregnancy-induced hypertension during the birth of their twin daughters. Emma's blood pressure had been so high and uncontrollable that she had irretrievably damaged both her kidneys. Three months later she had reached end-stage kidney failure and the thrice-weekly dialysis had been a constant juggling act.

If all went well, tomorrow's operation would return their shattered lives to some degree of normality and Emma and Peter were looking forward to more quality time with their daughters.

'A final day of work-up and then the big day.' Fergus looked across at Emma who smiled back weakly. His voice lowered. 'How are you, Emma?'

'Worried if anything happens to Peter.' Emma's eyes filled and she put her hand to her mouth so it was difficult to hear what she said.

Fergus bent towards her and tipped her chin up so she could see his smile. 'We'll be taking special care of him. Your Peter has three women who need him and I know he can't wait to see some colour in the cheeks of the woman he loves. Now, save some sympathy for yourself. You'll be under the anaesthetic longer than Peter and I want you to rest as much as you can today.'

Peter spoke from the next bed, where he was sitting fully dressed. He pointed to a picture of two chubby babies in matching pink outfits who grinned toothlessly out of the photo frame. 'My mum brought the girls in last night so they aren't coming in today.'

Fergus shook hands with him. 'How are you feeling, Peter? Nervous?'

Peter was dark-haired and serious. 'Perhaps a little,

but I'm excited, too. Emma and I are a team and half the team is out on her feet. Normally I can't keep up with her. I want Emma well.'

Ailee lowered her voice. 'Is your mum going to stay for a while to help with the children? You need to rest afterwards and you'll be pretty sore.'

'Yes.' Peter also spoke quietly. 'And my dad's taken over running the store. I worry about his heart condition but we just can't afford to close until I get well enough to go back.'

Fergus nodded and Ailee could see the frustration in his body language. 'That's where everything needs to change. Live donors save lives and save the government thousands of dollars in dialysis every year. Donors need their out-of-pocket expenses reimbursed. We're not talking about making a profit but to take away the hardship such a selfless act incurs.'

Peter sighed. 'Wouldn't that make it easier? But if it costs us our home, it's still worth it. We have to have Emma well again.'

'At least with the laparoscopic surgery that I use, your recovery time will be reduced by a few weeks. There will still be four small wounds, one for the laparoscopic camera on its cable to allow me vision for what I'm doing and two for the other instruments that will divide and separate your kidney from its bed. A fourth excision below the umbilicus will be made through which to remove the kidney.'

'It sounds so easy.' Peter rolled his eyes. 'Not!'

'There are still risks but we'll look after you and your wife.' Fergus rested his hand on Peter's shoulder.

'I'll come back tonight and answer any final questions about tomorrow and look at the last lot of results.'

'Maurice…' Fergus patted the pharmacist on the back '…is going to run through Emma's immunosuppressant regime again with you both so we're sure you understand how to help prevent her body rejecting your kidney and the side-effects she can expect. If there's anything else you don't understand, ask Ailee or any of the team, and we'll take some extra time to explain.'

The group moved on and Fergus seemed to have a rapport with every patient—much like the man she'd spent time with in Singapore. A totally different person to the one who glanced indifferently across at her now.

When the round was over, the team met in the foyer to discuss any further changes or additions that were needed, and then the group broke up.

'Dr Green?' Fergus spoke quietly but his voice carried effortlessly to her. 'I'd like to speak to you in the office.'

Ailee looked up at Fergus's request and met his eyes. Without saying a word she preceded him into the office and he closed the door behind them.

He gestured for her to sit down and Ailee shook her head. A discussion that needed a seat, she wasn't ready for. 'I don't have the time to sit down. What can I do for you, Mr McVicker?'

He stared at a point over her left shoulder. 'I apologise for being abrupt and only wish to make it clear you'll have no unwanted attention from me.'

Ailee glanced at the door, eager to get out of there and away from his presence. 'Thank you. Is that all? I gather you were expecting me?'

'Oh, I knew you were here. I won't single you out
again—unless you're late. That will be all, thank you,
Doctor.'

Ally cast one puzzled look at him and left the room.

Fergus watched her go, not sure he'd handled that well.

When she'd walked into the ward that morning, her
presence had punched him in the gut as it had the first
time he'd seen her, but he'd just have to get over that.

Listening to her talk to Jody and Peter had carried
him back to the way she'd been supportive on the plane
and in Singapore and, of course, later in his arms. He
didn't understand the different sides to her.

When Lionel Harry had asked him to cover him here,
he'd been trapped as he wasn't scheduled back at his
own hospital for a month and was the most likely replacement.

If he'd known Ailee worked here, he would have
flown a replacement in from overseas rather than come
himself. Unfortunately by the time he'd found out he'd
already agreed to come.

To top that off, Sophie hadn't been impressed that he'd
cancelled their holiday but he'd make it up to her. She
seemed pleased to be back home as a day student again.

His mind wandered back to Ailee, as it had several
times a day and most of the nights over the last week. He
was surprised their paths hadn't crossed before, considering how close their work was. Apparently she was a gifted
surgeon. He wouldn't have forgotten a previous meeting.

He'd since discovered she was well liked and re-
spected for her dedication to the renal transplant unit.

He didn't understand why she was temping in a transplant co-ordinator's job instead of getting on with resuming her position—but he would find out. Not that he'd be a fool again with this woman.

Ailee's day got steadily busier. She had a lecture on donor liaison with medical students at ten and it was five to the hour now.

All medical professionals needed to be skilled and empathetic when approaching bereaved families and learn how to discuss organ and tissue donation and her brain couldn't be distracted by thoughts of Fergus McVicker.

The lecture went well and her plug for all who attended to sign donor cards was well received, as was her point that anyone considering such a pledge should also make their family aware of it. This was one of the most common stumbling blocks between the original intent of the donor and the recipient life being saved.

Lunch was a snatched sandwich and just enough time to ask Rita, the charge nurse of the renal transplant unit, the burning question, 'How long is Fergus McVicker staying?'

'What's the story with you two?' Rita's bright blue eyes stared straight at Ailee and avoided Ailee's question.

Ailee raised her eyebrows and stared right back—a trick she'd learned from her brother when he was cornered. 'There's no story. He must have taken an instant dislike to me.'

Rita laughed. 'Nobody takes an instant dislike to you. Look at you! Care and empathy shine out of every gorgeous pore.'

'Please, Rita. Give me the good news.'

Rita shrugged and gave up. 'He's here for two weeks, maybe four. It all depends on Mrs Harry. She's improving well and she may visit their daughter for her convalescence, in which case Dr Harry will be back sooner.'

'So how could our Mr McVicker drop everything at Sydney West?'

'He was on holiday. Apparently he's got a daughter who isn't happy Daddy's taken on the job, though. He's a widower and unattached. He could be just your type, Ailee, when all this is over.'

Rita smiled and then her smile faded. 'How is William today? He must be pretty disappointed he got sick when you were due home. Is he psyched up for the op?'

'He's due in this afternoon for the assessment clinic. He's improved a lot and we'll both be glad when he's well again.'

The transplant assessment clinic was held every afternoon at one o'clock. The renal team reviewed the suitability of end-stage renal patients for transplantation.

Again, when Ailee arrived at the ward, two minutes early, everyone else was already assembled. She saw Fergus glance at the clock and she was glad she wasn't late.

Obviously he had a fetish for punctuality. She'd make sure he didn't have anything to complain about and vowed she'd turn up fifteen minutes before everyone else next session.

William was the first patient and when Fergus picked up the chart his brow furrowed as he read the name. Green. How ironic. She wasn't just standing in front of him. Reminders of Ailee seem to be every-where. Even patients had the same name. He had it bad. It was a pity she wasn't worth the angst. He shut the thoughts off.

'Hello, William. I see you've just been through a tough patch but are improving steadily now?'

'I'm getting there.' He was a tall boy and there was something familiar about him that Fergus couldn't quite pin down. He'd probably seen him at Sydney West renal unit but it wasn't like him to forget a face.

'So you have this week and next week in the assessment clinic to finalise dates for your transplant. I see you've come in consistently over your fluid limit. Let's get you examined and we'll answer any questions you have because I expect your operation could be as early as Monday week if you continue to improve.'

Rita pulled the curtains and the rest of the team stepped back.

So Fergus hadn't connected William with her. Ailee felt guilty that she hadn't told him but, considering how unfriendly he'd been to her, he didn't deserve to know anyway. Maybe if she had told him why she'd left he wouldn't be treating her like this. She'd never know.

Today had been huge, considering all that was happening. Her new job, running into Fergus, William coming in for assessment to set the date for their operations—it was no wonder her head was spinning.

'Are you OK?' Maurice was beside her and his face showed concern.

'I'm fine. Sorry. I suppose I just realised how dangerous the op is for William.'

'William isn't the only person who's having an operation.'

Ailee shook her head. 'Mine's nothing. A bit of discomfort, a scar, and I'll be just as healthy at the end. William has the drugs to live with for the rest of his life.'

'And a much better life he'll have, thanks to you.'

Ailee frowned at Maurice and there was no doubt his look held particular warmth. More complications. She felt a hundred years older than Maurice but he was probably only a year or two younger than she was. Although he was a nice lad, he seemed so young and immature—especially after Singapore. Already Fergus had spoiled other men for her.

The curtains were pulled back and her eyes were drawn as the man in her thoughts stared straight into her face.

There was a moment's silence and for a second she thought he'd discovered William was her brother and he was going to take her arm and steer her into the office again. Her heart pounded in her chest.

Two trips to the office would start a gossip storm. But he didn't.

He just moved on.

CHAPTER FIVE

By Wednesday Ailee had found her feet in her new job. Each new challenge served to increase her respect for her predecessor and for the whole renal team.

At the top of her list, surprisingly, was Fergus McVicker, tireless in his pursuit of optimum health for his patients and demanding high standards from all on the team. The fact that he received unqualified support from everyone he came into contact with was because of his own dedication.

The patients adored him and Ailee found it hard to comprehend that she had shared such intimacy with this driven man.

Superficially she appeared the most immune out of the staff to seeing Fergus almost every day. Unfortunately she couldn't help the jump in her heart rate or ache in her chest when she was near him, and she sometimes wondered if she would go quietly insane for wanting some of their closeness to return. If only William's operation could be scheduled sooner and she could try to salvage some rapport from their past association. But life wasn't like that.

An hour after the assessment clinic Ailee's pager went off.

The call originated from Intensive Care to call her for donor liaison. ICU had a family who hadn't known their dying daughter had signed a donor card. The girl's parents were naturally having trouble coming to terms with her wish to donate her organs.

Ailee's stomach fluttered at the thought of the hours ahead. Her input could make such a difference to their decision, many people's lives and especially the donor family's grieving process, and she was anxious to do her best.

When Ailee arrived at the intensive care unit, Andrew, an anaesthetist she'd worked with the previous year, handed her the second set of brain-stem death tests from the unfortunate young woman.

'Hi, Ailee. Good to see you back, but not in these circumstances. I have a tragedy here for you. Twenty-five-year-old Eva Ellis was involved in a car accident and never regained consciousness.' They both looked towards the separate room adjacent to the desk.

Andrew went on. 'Her parents are with her.' His pager went off and he glanced down at the screen. 'I have to go.' He patted Ailee on the back. 'Good luck.'

Eva's parents were sitting beside the bed, holding their daughter's hand, and Ailee went over to the nurse who was specialling Eva on the ventilator.

The machine breathed and hissed mechanically to provide oxygen to a person who would never recover or ever be able to breathe or think for herself. The tragedy was enormous.

'I'm Ailee Green, the transplant co-ordinator.'

The nurse was very young but remarkably composed. 'It's Dr Green, isn't it? I'm Sam, the family are waiting to speak to you. I told them you'd be here soon. I'll introduce you.'

Sam took Ailee across to the grieving parents. 'Excuse me, Mr and Mrs Ellis. This is Dr Green. She is the transplant co-ordinator we spoke about.'

A grief-ravaged woman in her early fifties held out her hand and her fingers were shaking in Ailee's grip. 'I'm Marion and this is my husband, John.'

Ailee squeezed the woman's hand. 'I'm Ailee. I'm so sorry to have to meet you like this and intrude on your grief at this time. The fact that your daughter has signed and carried a donor card tells us a little about how special a person she was. I know this is very hard to discuss but I will try to keep it as simple as possible.'

Marion nodded and Ailee went on. 'I understand you and your husband didn't know that Eva had signed a donor card?'

Both parents shook their head.

'So you were shocked?'

Marion nodded. 'It wasn't something we'd ever talked about. Now, seeing Eva like this, it would be like killing our own daughter to give away her organs. We don't know what to do.'

'I can see how you think that.' Ailee reached out and took Marion's hand. Her voice was very soft and very gentle. 'You both know that the person you knew as Eva, your daughter, has gone. She can't ever come back except in your memories. Her brain has suffered such a loss of oxygen that it cannot even tell her body to breathe for her. If the machine wasn't inflating her lungs, she would have died hours ago.'

Ailee stopped to let her words sink in. She couldn't imagine the pain these parents must be going through at this moment, and for a second she doubted she could control her own emotions.

Then she thought of Jody—a young woman with her whole life ahead of her, except she'd needed a new kidney and pancreas—and how the incredible gift bestowed by her donor and their family had changed her life. Surely it was unnecessary to waste Eva's perfectly functioning organs when Eva herself had seen the value in the concept.

'To give you some idea, we had a young woman on our transplant ward who went home this week. She is a wonderfully intelligent young woman, much like I imagine your daughter was, and has a lovely sense of humour. A month ago she was going to die because her kidneys had both stopped working and dialysis was making her sicker. She has had severe diabetes since she was ten.'

Ailee paused to see if they were following the story.

'On Monday she went home with not only a new kidney but a new pancreas as well. Amazingly, she isn't even a diabetic now. This young woman's life is possible because of wonderful people like you and your daughter who have made the decision to donate their organs after they have died.'

'Does the donor—' Marion stumbled over the word '—family, get to meet the person who has their relative's organs?'

'Not usually. But this woman I mentioned is writing a letter that I will pass on to the family. Of all the people who know what a huge thing this is for the donor family to agree to, the recipients are the most aware. They actually find it very hard to get over how fortunate they are.'

Marion nodded and turned to her husband who nodded back. 'Eva was a very caring person. She would hate to think we wasted her organs when she didn't need them any more.'

John spoke for the first time. 'We can't let our little girl down on this, Marion.' The balding man's eyes were brimming with tears. 'It's what she wanted and it's the last thing we can do for our baby.'

'If you both agree, Eva's donation will help a lot of people—not just one or two. In a week or so I will let you know just how much your daughter's donation is going to change the lives of so many people.'

Marion blew her nose and sniffed. 'How does it happen and will you be there?'

'I won't be in the actual operation room but I will be co-ordinating from the outside. I can arrange for you to speak to someone who will be at the operation, though.'

Marion looked at her husband and he nodded. 'Yes. Please. I think we need that.'

'I'll arrange that. We also need to know if there are any organs or tissue restrictions you would like me to pass on to the transplant team. Some people do have restrictions and we respect that.'

Marion looked across at John and he shook his head slowly. 'They can take whatever will help someone else.

The real essence of our daughter is at rest—she doesn't need her body any more.'

'I'll come back this evening after I've organised the teams and set up the paperwork. We need to have blood taken for tissue-typing and other checks and we need to know if your daughter had any illnesses and about her general health.'

Ailee contacted the transplant data office and the patient's details were entered. The computer assimilated the information and allocated the organs to those most in need and who were compatible.

There was one phone call she was dreading. She'd run through who on the transplant or harvest team she would contact to meet Eva's parents, and the most obvious choice was the man in charge.

Ailee had no doubt that despite Fergus's behaviour towards her at the moment, he would be a very caring advocate to introduce to the grieving parents.

'Mr McVicker? It's Ailee Green. I'm sorry to bother you at your surgery but I have a favour to ask.'

'Yes, Ailee?' There was an expectant note in his voice but she was too anxious to try and figure it out.

'The family of the young woman donor that came in today would like to speak to someone who will be present during the operation. Would you speak to them for me, please, before you scrub?'

'Of course. I'll meet them in ICU at seven. Is that all?'

Ailee sighed with relief. 'Yes, thanks,' she said, and as she tried to put the phone down she realised she'd have to consciously release her fingers because she'd been gripping the receiver far too fiercely.

The afternoon passed swiftly and it had been dark for an hour when Ailee returned with Fergus to the parents.

'This is Mr McVicker. He's the renal surgeon and in charge at the moment of the transplants in this hospital.'

Fergus shook hands with Marion and John. 'Please, accept my sincere sympathy for the loss of your daughter and the difficult situation you are in.'

Marion nodded and Fergus went on, 'I want you to know that the operation is performed with every respect and dignity by each of the very experienced transplant teams who will come to our hospital.'

Eva's parents nodded. 'The operations can take between six and eight hours and are carried out as sterile operations, of course. Afterwards we do repair any incisions we make.'

Fergus answered a few more questions and then it was time for him to go to Theatre.

Marion and John went once more into Intensive Care and then they were ready to leave. 'So we will be able to see Eva's body after the operation?'

Ailee nodded. 'Tomorrow morning I'll come and take you to our chapel in the mortuary, where you can spend as much time as you wish.'

'Thank you, Ailee.'

'Thank you. You have made the right decision. We all appreciate your kindness in following this through during your immense grief. Your daughter's legacy will live on through those she helps.'

'We know. It's just hard to think of it at the moment.' Marion squeezed her husband's hand and Ailee bit her lip.

'Of course. This isn't the time to worry about that. Please, try and get some rest. I'll see you in the morning. It was what Eva wanted and it takes courage to make this decision.'

Marion looked sadly at Ailee. 'We don't feel brave, just heartbroken.'

Ailee watched them walk away arm in arm, leaning on each other, and she felt tears well into her eyes. She brushed her hand across her face as she tried to contain her tears, at least until she reached the safety of her office, but as she pushed open the door the heartbreak over-whelmed her.

'I knew you'd be upset,' he said softly.

Fergus leant against the wall and pushed himself off when she entered. He held open his arms and her brain said no as her heart steered her into the comfort of his embrace. She sobbed quietly for a minute or two to ease the strain of staying strong for the last few hours, and he just held her gently until the storm was over.

Despite her tears, she did feel better and Ailee lifted her ravaged face to thank him, but that thought caught and died as they stared at each other. There was nothing either of them could do as a force greater than their wills drew them together for a single, healing kiss.

'No.' Ailee stepped back out of his arms and her hand came up to cover her mouth. 'You said you wouldn't.'

'I did, didn't I?' Fergus looked at her and she couldn't read the expression on his face. 'I'm sorry,' he said, and walked out of the office. She felt like crying again, for a different reason.

The next morning, Thursday, when Ailee went to meet Marion and John to take them to the mortuary, Fergus was with them. He had his arm around Marion, whose face was streaked with tears.

Fergus looked as if he'd had twelve hours' sleep, instead of having operated all night, and only the lines around his eyes betrayed his tiredness. As Ailee came closer there was no weariness in his voice.

'You can ring my surgery if you have any other questions and I'll phone you back as soon as I can.'

He looked up. His eyes darkened with concern when he saw Ailee, as if he knew how hard this was for her, and she was transported back to their kiss yesterday. Then he looked away and she felt cold. How did he do that?

Fergus spoke to the bereaved parents. 'Here's Dr Green. I have to go.' He shook hands with John and to Ailee's surprise hugged Marion again. 'It's been a privilege meeting you both.'

They all watched Fergus move away and John reached over and took his wife's hand. He looked at Ailee and then the sign that pointed the way to the chapel. 'Let's say goodbye to our daughter, love.'

By the time Ailee had made it back to the ward she felt emotionally shattered by sharing Marion and John's grief again.

After the last twenty-four hours she admired the injured Maureen, the woman she was replacing at the moment, more than ever to be able to constantly deal with such emotive issues day in and day out as a transplant co-ordinator.

As soon as she walked into the ward her pager went off, just as Rita appeared breathlessly beside her.

'Ailee.' Rita gulped air. 'Mr McVicker is looking for you. The page is from the operating theatres. Emma is bleeding and they need more help. The extra team had to leave and are tied up in a critical trauma case down in Emergency. Fergus wants to know if you can assist in Theatre Six.'

Ailee felt her stomach drop at the thought of Emma with a major haemorrhage. 'Answer the page. I'm on my way.'

Ailee turned and ran out the door. She didn't bother waiting for the lifts. It was only two flights and the stairwell came out beside the operating suite. She'd surgically assisted Dr Harry there for twelve months before going off to Scotland and she knew the way.

Ailee pushed through the plastic doors. Ominously, there was no one in the reception area. Obviously everyone was caught up with the emergency. She slipped into the change room and changed into her theatre scrubs faster than she'd ever done in her life.

When she entered the scrub room, a spare gown and two pairs of gloves were waiting for her, and before she'd finished drying her hands the scout nurse came in to tie her gown.

'What's happening?' Ailee struggled with her gloves while the nurse finished tying her gown.

'The transplanted kidney was seated and blood supply established and everything was routine. The other surgeon left for the emergency downstairs but then Mr McVicker suspected a hidden bleeder and the new registrar hasn't enough experience to cope.

'Mr McVicker asked for help and the anaesthetist— you know how Andrew likes to bend the rules—said there was no one else except you. The kidney is at risk let alone the patient.'

'Nice to be the last hope.' Ailee was finished and spun around to enter the theatre.

'You had our vote.' The nurse glanced through the window into the theatre to make sure the way was clear for the sterile-gowned Ailee to enter.

'You're finally here.' Fergus looked up and his expression appeared grim.

'What can I do?' Ailee answered calmly as she stood beside the shaking registrar and peered into the wound that was awash with bright blood.

'I need some vision through this blood and with only two of us we don't have enough hands.'

'I'll take the sucker.' Ailee spoke to the registrar who thankfully handed over the plastic nozzle. 'You take the retractor and pull from that angle with two hands. It will be easier now.'

'More swabs.' Fergus was concentrating and Ailee slid them across from the scrub sister, who looked pale under her eye shield as she hurried to do what she was told.

'And can I have a swab on a stick as well, please?' Ailee's gentle voice seemed to dissipate the tension in the room. Ailee swabbed the area she'd just suctioned and for a brief instant a welling of blood could be isolated from the rest before it disappeared under a tide of red that filled the cavity again.

'Good work, Ailee.' Fergus had seen it, too, and now that he knew where the problem lay, he set to isolating the vessel as fast as he could.

'Blood pressure's going through the floor.' Andrew's voice drifted laconically to the surgeons as he set about increasing the amount of fluid he was infusing. 'I'm on the last packed cells now.'

'I can see the bleeder.' Fergus acknowledged he'd heard the warning. 'I won't be long and we'll stop wasting the stuff.'

The alarms sounded from the anaesthetic equipment and Ailee spared a brief thought for Peter and Emma's baby girls if Emma's lack of blood caused her to go into cardiac arrest on the table. It was a horrific scenario to contemplate. She forced away the thought. The situation was grim but she didn't doubt that Fergus would gain control. He had almost finished repairing the vessel, and Ailee had never seen one ligated so well under such circumstances. 'That was quick, but there's still too much blood.'

'Then find where it's coming from, fast.' Fergus finished his knot and held his hand out for another suture.

Ailee spoke to the registrar. 'Can you pull from a more lateral angle? I want to see under the bladder.'

For the briefest moment, after suctioning and a quick

swipe with the swab at the end of the long forceps, Ailee spotted another mini-fountain of blood. That explained it and she knew they'd win the battle now.

'I saw it and I've got it.' Fergus pressed his finger on the spot and collected another swab from the scrub sister. 'You little bastard,' he said softly.

Ailee raised her eyebrows. 'Language.'

The registrar looked doubtfully at Ailee taking on the boss, especially after the morning he'd had.

Fergus glanced up in time to see her censure and his eyes crinkled as he relaxed. 'Smack me later.'

Andrew looked up and then adjusted another gauge on his machine as he coughed to hide his amusement. 'So are you people going to be long?'

Fergus had tied off the last of the rogue vessels. 'Closing now.'

Over the next ten minutes Emma's blood pressure crept up and the abdominal layers were closed without further setbacks. Ailee stepped back as the final closure began and stripped off her gloves.

'Thank you, Dr Green.' Fergus didn't take his eyes off the patient but his voice raised the awareness between them.

'My pleasure, Mr McVicker.'

She smiled at the registrar. 'Well done, Tom. It's all good experience afterwards, isn't it?' Ailee stripped off her outer gown to leave the bloodstained clothing in the theatre. She waved at Andrew and smiled at each person in the room except Fergus before she pushed open the door. 'Bye, everybody.'

Ailee didn't go back to the ward. She sat in her office

and pretended to do paperwork as her mind kept going over the crisis in Theatre.

To lose Emma would have been a tragedy, and it had been close. Fergus had been exceptional, very talented. The bleeder had been no one's fault and the spotting of it before closure would have made the difference to trying to retrieve an irretrievable situation if they'd missed it.

When William's transplant was over she would be able to go back to what she loved doing. Surgery was something she was skilled at and there would always be hospitals to take her. Dr Harry had already offered her tenure, working with an eye to a consultancy in the not-too-distant future.

The problem was now that she'd worked with Fergus, it would seem flat. From only that brief window she'd seen skills that she hoped to emulate one day.

She picked up the phone. There was work to do before the round.

Fergus knew the moment Ailee arrived on the ward. He tried not to glance her way but it was hard, especially after yesterday's kiss.

He'd been amazed at her quiet confidence and skill in Theatre and attributed a lot of the retrieval of Emma's haemorrhage to Ailee's help. He had to admit Ailee was a good woman to have by his side in a crisis.

Before coming to Theatre she'd already had a tough morning, being there to support Eva's grieving parents again.

It was funny how he might not think much of her sensitivity in Singapore, but he had no doubt she'd give everything in her work.

Which reminded him, considering her undoubted skill in surgery, it was even more ludicrous she was temping as a co-ordinator.

Maybe she was temporary at everything? He had to ask Rita, the unit manager, when he had a chance.

Peter was back from his operation, still groggy from the anaesthetic and pain relief.

He opened his eyes and squinted up at Fergus. 'How's Emma, Doc?'

'Emma's doing well. She lost more blood than we anticipated but she's fine now. She'll stay in Intensive Care tonight and High Dependency tomorrow. It all looks good so far. How are you feeling?'

Peter almost smiled. 'Sore. Glad it's over.' His eyelids drooped and his voice faded. Then he forced his eyes open again. 'You're sure Emma's OK?'

'She's fine. Rest and recover. She'll be just as anxious about you when she comes back to the ward.'

Fergus rubbed his eyes. They felt scratchy with lack of sleep and twelve hours of surgery. He'd head home for the rest of the morning and catch a couple of hours' shut-eye before the afternoon surgery.

When Fergus opened his eyes, Ailee had come up to the group and her concerned look tore at the fabric of his control. He'd love to rest his head on her. 'Yes, Ailee?' His voice came out much sharper than he'd intended in a knee-jerk reaction to his own weakness.

He watched her recoil from the harshness in his tone and he winced. 'I'm sorry.' Now he just sounded gruff.

Lord, what this woman was doing to his emotions. 'Did you want something?'

'There's a call for you. Rita asked me to pass the message on.'

An excuse to leave! Fergus grabbed at the chance. 'I'll come now. After the round, if you have to contact me, I'll be at home. Ring me there.'

Ailee nodded and turned away to answer a question from Maurice about a new patient who'd just arrived.

Ailee was glad of the distraction because she was becoming more annoyed all the time about Fergus and the way he reacted to her. In fact, she'd skip the rest of the round because there was no further need for her here today.

Anyone would think she had done something wrong when all she could be accused of was being attracted to a man she'd met on a plane. What gave him the right to pass judgement on her?

He was treating her like a scarlet woman, even after their brief affinity in Theatre.

Well, it took two to tango and Fergus McVicker had been just as abandoned in Singapore before his daughter had phoned. And he'd initiated that kiss yesterday, not her.

Ailee bit her lip and closed her eyes briefly. This was not the place to recall those memories. Her cheeks warmed and she felt the tears prick the backs of her eyes. This was ridiculous. And to think she'd considered chasing the man up after William was well again.

She drew a deep breath and lifted her head. There were a hundred things to do and she'd better get started.

The patient Maurice wanted her to see was an elderly lady who was almost but not quite at the dialysis stage.

'I wondered if you had time to explain haemodialysis again to Agnes, please, Ailee. I came to explain her medications but she doesn't understand dialysis and I know how good you are at explanations.'

Maurice turned to a seventy-ish white-haired woman whose lined face mapped years of laughter.

'This is Dr Green, Agnes.'

Ailee warmed to her immediately and held out her hand.

'Hello, Agnes. I'm Ailee. Maurice says you have some questions about haemodialysis.'

'Haemo-whatever.' The old lady snorted. 'I suppose it would help if I could remember what to call the darned thing, but what I really want to know is how my blood can go into some machine dirty and come out clean without killing me.'

Ailee grinned. 'If it was my blood, I'd want to know, too.' She sat down beside Agnes.

'You know, Agnes, with your increasing renal failure, the amount of water you are passing is getting less and less.'

'Hmmph,' said Agnes. 'And that's a good thing as I don't have to get up at night to pee, finally.'

Ailee shook her head. 'It will keep getting less until you might only pass an eggcup full of urine in twenty-four hours. That's not good.'

'Why not?' Agnes was concentrating.

'Because any extra fluids you swallow can't leave your body until the next three-times-a-week dialysis can remove it.'

Ailee went on. 'Too much extra fluid causes oedema,

or water in your tissues, like swollen ankles, which puts a load on your heart. Your heart will blow up like a balloon to cope with the extra fluid and then deflate when they take the fluid off. All that stretching and deflating weakens your heart as well.'

Agnes nodded slowly. 'So it's the fluid that's the problem?'

Ailee smiled. Agnes was catching on fast. 'Not just the fluid. Your kidneys are like a filter in a coffee-machine. They collect the impurities from your blood and send the wastes out in the urine. If your kidneys don't work, they won't do that and your body fills up with toxins.'

Agnes nodded and Ailee went on. 'The haemodialysis is your artificial kidney. You weigh yourself before being connected to the machine and your weight determines how much extra fluid needs to be removed while your blood is being cleaned.'

Agnes frowned. 'And if I don't have this haemo-whatever, I just die from the poisons and fluid that build up in my body that I can't get rid of on my own.'

'Dialysis saves people's lives,' Ailee agreed, 'but still at best only provides fifteen per cent of what is called "normal" kidney function.'

'So I have to stay on the piddly amount of fluid I'm allowed to drink. Four cups or so only?'

'I'm afraid so. It can cause cramps if you drink too much and the machine has to take the extra out of your blood.'

'So how does the blood go in and out? Do they put a tap in or something?'

'Something like that,' Ailee said. 'Before you start

treatment, one of our doctors will put a shunt in your arm…' Ailee pointed to a spot halfway between Agnes's hand and her elbow '…where they will connect you to the machine with a needle each time.'

Agnes rubbed her wrist at the thought. 'So how does this coffee-machine clean my blood, or have you told me that bit and I didn't get it?'

'No, I'm slow but I'll get there.' The two women smiled at each other and Ailee went on. 'Dialysis is a lot to take in at one time and we'll go over it again at each stage.'

'Give me the good news,' Agnes snorted.

'Your blood is pumped through a plastic cylinder that contains thousands of very fine tubes. Each tube has tiny holes that let the waste and extra fluid pass through but not the blood cells or protein. A special fluid washes around the outside of the tubes so that your blood can be returned to you with the toxins removed.'

'So how long do I have to stay tied to the machine with a needle in my arm?'

'It takes about four hours for all your blood to pass through the machine about six times.'

'Blimey. And to think I never appreciated my kidneys.'

Ailee grinned. 'That's what I learnt when I came to work here.'

Agnes scratched her chin and the hair poking out under her lip wobbled. 'OK, dearie. I'd say my old brain's done as well as it can.'

'It's a pretty heavy topic,' Ailee agreed, 'but each time you come, ask more questions. Everyone is happy to help you understand what is happening. Good luck.'

Agnes had restored Ailee's sense of humour and she headed back to her own office happier and without glancing at Fergus as he completed the round. Unfortunately, she could still feel his gaze on the back of her neck all the way up the corridor.

By Friday Fergus was losing his battle to remain aloof with Ailee. Since that time in Theatre she'd never been far from his thoughts.

He woke in the morning dreaming of her back in his arms and at work he felt every smile she gave so freely to all except him. This was crazy. He'd have to do something soon or he'd crack.

'Dr Green? Ailee?' Fergus caught up just as Ailee came to the entrance of the renal ward. She jumped and put her hand to her chest as if he'd leapt out in front of her.

Fergus frowned. 'I'm sorry. I didn't mean to startle you.'

He watched her take a deep, calming breath and unconsciously his hand lifted to lie on her arm in reassurance.

When she looked down at his fingers on her skin he felt his own gaze drawn as well. It was as if they were both back in Singapore and finally he had an inkling she was just as affected by his proximity as he was by hers.

'We need to talk.' His words came out with more overtones than he'd intended, but it was a measure of his relief that he had no control over his voice.

Why hadn't he noticed this before? He wanted to back her into a corner of the ward, put his arms on either side of her head—trap her so she couldn't escape—and find out then and there why she had really run away that morning.

Slowly her head came up and she met his look with a fierce one of her own. 'Is it about a patient?'

'No!'

'Then I'm busy.' She glared at him but he didn't believe her this time.

CHAPTER SIX

UNDER her bravado Fergus could feel Ailee's indecision and he stepped closer. 'Give me a time and we'll talk then.'

Fergus suspected if he didn't pin her down now he would have trouble cornering her again. She hesitated and he pounced. 'No is not an option,' he said quietly.

She didn't answer so he solved it for her. 'Then we will make it this afternoon when you finish.'

Ailee shook her head. 'I have a family dinner at seven.'

'No problem. I'll pick you up at five from here and we'll find somewhere private then I'll drop you back.'

'Not too private.' Her voice was dry and she looked composed but he had the feeling she wasn't as cool as she seemed.

'As you wish,' he said, and watched her nod and turn to walk away from him. He just hoped he hadn't been mistaken about his instinct or he was going to look even more of a fool.

Ailee sensed Fergus behind her shoulder, even though he wasn't touching her, and they entered the ward together. Rita raised her eyebrows at the tension between them but thankfully the unit manager didn't make one of her usual teasing comments.

The ward had a new patient today and soon all attention centred on Lawrence Roper.

Lawrence had needed a kidney transplant after going into renal failure a year ago and, because he was an orphan and a single man, and the average waiting time in Australia for a donated kidney was four years, sometimes longer, he had decided not to wait.

With commercial transplantation prohibited in Australia, the United Kingdom and the United States, he'd sold his house and used the money to go overseas and purchase a black-market kidney from a country with a commercial programme giving donors monetary compensation.

This alternative to waiting had proved to be a sometimes dangerous option for those who chose it, and it certainly seemed so for Lawrence.

Fergus shook the patient's hand. 'Good morning, Lawrence.'

The man was in his late twenties, dark-haired and unwell-looking. 'Hello again, Doc. Bet you didn't expect to see me again.'

'No. I'm sorry you're not well, old son.' Fergus turned to the team with a wry smile. 'Lawrence was over at Sydney West and decided to not wait for the donor programme. He went for broke—literally.'

He smiled at the young man and Ailee admired Fergus's non-judgemental attitude of Lawrence's choices.

Fergus went on. 'Lawrence travelled to another country six months ago and when he returned to Australia post-transplant he was well. Now he's become concerned that his condition has deteriorated.'

He glanced down at the report in his hand. 'We've brought him in to fine-tune his medication regime, stabilise any damage if we can, and follow up a few of his concerns.'

He lowered his voice. 'I've got your blood tests back and I'm afraid it is what you suspected. You contracted a blood-borne disease from your donor or the equipment during the procedure.'

Lawrence closed his eyes and sank back in the bed. 'You warned me.'

Fergus turned to Ailee. 'Lawrence's condition has been complicated by contracting hepatitis B, despite his surgeon's assurance his donor had been screened. He'll need help with information and support so he can come to terms with that.'

'I suppose I can be glad it's not AIDS, but hepatitis B can be pretty rotten, too, can't it?' Lawrence managed to smile whimsically at Ailee.

Ailee was impressed with how philosophical the young man appeared. She leaned towards him and touched his shoulder. 'I'll have the communicable disease sister come and see you, Lawrence. Trudy can answer any questions and concerns that you have, as well as connect you to some support so you don't feel as isolated as you do now.'

Fergus nodded. 'When we sort out your medications, you'll feel better as well. Give yourself a few days to get over the shock and we'll have you as well as you can be before you leave.'

'Thanks, Doc.' Lawrence held out his hand. Fergus shook it and then rested his hand on the young man's shoulder for a moment before moving on.

Ailee could tell that Fergus was affected by Lawrence's plight.

'It's a sad twist for him,' she said. Personal issues were forgotten for the moment.

Fergus met Ailee's eyes. 'It's a tragedy. Five of the last sixteen patients that I know of who have gone overseas have died within twelve months. Contracting a blood-borne disease because of inadequate screening is one of the major causes of complications following commercial transplants.'

He compressed his lips. 'The tragedy is that if we could lift our national donor rate to where it is in progressive places like South Australia, Lawrence wouldn't have been driven to take the risks he had.'

Ailee nodded because she couldn't agree more. They desperately needed to raise public awareness for participation in the donor programme. Ailee was glad that Fergus felt as strongly as she did because donor promotion was dear to her heart.

The hours flew by but Ailee couldn't get the resignation in Lawrence's face out of her mind. She supposed it was a mixed blessing as Lawrence distracted her from worrying about her appointment with Fergus later that day.

As the clock crept around to five, Ailee put off her coming meeting with Fergus, and she dropped back to sit for a few minutes at the side of Lawrence's bed. 'How are you going, Lawrence?'

'I'm not too bad.' He looked at Ailee's handbag. 'Going home?' He smiled at Ailee. 'Mr McVicker said you're a doctor?'

'Yep. I'm Transplant co-ordinator at the moment but I'm just filling in. How did you go with Trudy? Did she answer your questions about hepatitis B?'

Lawrence's eyes lit up. 'She's a special lady. You all are. She's coming back to see me again tomorrow. I thought everyone would think I was such a loser for going overseas and then being stupid enough to get burned.'

'I'm sure your reasons were good.'

He raised his eyebrows comically but Ailee could see no humour in his sad blue eyes. 'Yeah. If I didn't go I wouldn't be here. Four years on dialysis wasn't for me.'

He shrugged. 'I kept getting sick, and I couldn't handle being put on and off the donor programme.'

He shook his head. 'Then I'd get depressed and have a few days on the booze. When I came into dialysis I'd be way overloaded in fluid. The cramps would kill me when they had to draw off the extra fluid. So I thought I'd speed the process up and go for a commercial kidney. I wish I'd just done what I was told and waited.'

He sighed. 'It was a gamble but I wouldn't have made the four years anyway.'

Ailee's gaze sharpened. 'Was it that bad?'

He shrugged again. 'Not enough to live for.'

Ailee shook her head vehemently. 'There's always enough to live for.'

'Spoken like a woman in charge of her life.' Lawrence smiled grimly. 'I don't have family, I can't work because I've been sick for two years, my friends feel bad when they're well and I'm not. It's not much fun and I don't see the point.'

Ailee disagreed. 'I don't see that. Everyone can make a difference. Lawrence, you have experiences that new end-stage kidney-disease sufferers could learn from. Promise me you'll give me a chance to help you help them.'

'You sound like Mr McVicker.' Lawrence mocked her. 'He was always going on about what I had to offer. I reckon I would have topped myself a year ago if it wasn't for Mr McVicker.'

Ailee refused to give up. 'That proves you're special. I have to go, but I'll make a few enquiries, talk to some colleagues, and I'll see you tomorrow as well.'

She rested her hand on his shoulder and left. She could feel the stinging in her throat for the sadness around Lawrence.

He didn't have a sister who would donate her kidney and she wondered if she'd missed the times when William and all the other dialysis patients felt like Lawrence did. Depression could play such a large part in end-stage kidney disease and dialysis patients.

She was so absorbed in Lawrence's dilemma that she almost walked into Fergus. But she couldn't miss the man when he stood in front of her.

Ailee looked up as he smiled down into her face. For a moment all she could do was bask in the gentleness in his eyes. She recognised that look and the way it made her feel. Something had changed between them today and suddenly it was dangerous around Fergus again.

Rita came out of her office and Fergus looked away.

She opened her mouth to say something, looked at them both and then suddenly, inexplicably, she turned around and walked away.

Ailee blinked and could have kicked herself. She'd been mooning like a dairy cow in heat and the warmth of embarrassment ran up her cheeks.

Time alone with Fergus was a very bad idea. She'd forgotten the whole reason she'd backed away in Singapore. Lawrence's situation should have reminded her like nothing else could.

Fergus took Ailee's arm. 'Don't say it. You're coming with me before you change your mind.'

Ailee found herself marching beside Fergus like a new army recruit. Slowly her mind cleared and she realised what she was doing.

'Do you mind?' She shook off his hand and rubbed her arm. She was awake now and it was more important than ever to not become involved with Fergus.

'I thought you might have bolted,' he replied mildly.

'Was that an option?' she said dryly. 'I'm only here because the air needs clearing and I don't want this to happen again. You need to realise that.'

Fergus ignored what Ailee had considered a good response under pressure. 'We'll talk when I can give you my full attention,' was all he said.

He stopped beside a bottle-green Jaguar, long and sleek with a waft of new leather when he opened the door for her.

She narrowed her eyes at him and wondered if she might after all manage to not do this. He stared back and she accepted her escape wasn't in his plans.

Well, capitulation wasn't in hers either and she would choose her battleground.

Ailee sat ungraciously in the passenger seat and he closed the door with a satisfied slam. She clenched her hands nervously and then carefully straightened her fingers so he wouldn't see. She was darned if she'd let him know he put her on edge.

She lifted her chin when he was settled. 'Where are we going?'

Fergus glanced at her before he started the car. 'You don't want to be alone and I want to be private so we're going to my house. My housekeeper and her husband are there and my daughter won't be home for another two hours because of her self-defence class.'

Ailee laughed without mirth. 'I need self-defence to stop people forcing me into cars against my will.'

His lips twitched and she realised she hadn't seen him smile much since Singapore. 'I didn't force you— I just leant a little.' He looked across at her as he started the car. 'I'll take you home any time you ask.'

She opened her mouth but before she could speak he butted in to qualify his statement. 'As soon as we've had our talk.'

Ailee closed her mouth again, but strangely she did believe his promise. It should have reassured her.

They didn't speak during the short drive, though surprisingly the silence wasn't awkward. When they pulled into the sweeping drive past remote-controlled gates, Ailee remembered she'd met this man in first class on a plane, and that he came from a different world to her.

'You have a beautiful home.' At least his wealth showed he committed to the responsibilities of his job because he was passionate about his work and not because he needed the money.

The imposing white-columned building was surrounded by acres of manicured lawns and a high stone wall that prevented those on the outside from looking in.

'It was my mother's house, and before you ask, yes, I did have a mother.'

'Would I say that?' Suddenly she felt ridiculously at ease with him. Maybe it was just because they were away from the hospital, but the warmth in his eyes told her he could feel it, too.

He smiled. 'You would say anything if I made you wild enough.'

Ailee tossed her hair. 'I don't get that wild.'

His eyes darkened and his voice dropped. 'I've seen you wild.'

Suddenly their laughter disappeared and the silence in the car felt like a wind tunnel that sucked Ailee's strength away until she felt she could barely lift her head.

Fergus dragged in a breath and tore his eyes away from her face. 'Come inside,' he said.

He climbed out, walked round the car then opened her door, and she accepted his help, powerless to resist.

Fergus kept hold of her arm as she stood up. He didn't say anything as they walked towards the front door but his touch on her burned and her surroundings faded.

An elderly woman in an apron opened the door and Ailee smiled.

'This is my housekeeper, Martha. Martha, Dr Ailee Green.'

Martha and Ailee shook hands briefly. 'Fergus has mentioned you and your husband.'

'Aye. And he's mentioned you, too,' Martha said. 'I've put tea in the library, Fergus. Ring if you want me.'

'We'll be there in a moment.' Fergus ignored the lift of Martha's brows as he steered Ailee across the black and white tiled entry and past an open carved wooden door.

Ailee looked into the room as they went by and saw a round table with cups, a teapot and a basket of tiny cakes.

'Was that the library?' Ailee craned her neck.

He didn't answer and his hand moved to the small of her back as they arrived at the bottom of the stairs.

Ailee had the first flutter of panic as they ascended and Fergus didn't look at her as they reached the next floor.

'We'll have tea in a moment.' He stopped in front of another closed door and turned the handle, indicating she should precede him into the room.

A moment… She swallowed and tried to settle her heart rate with that tiny reassurance—surely not a lot could happen in a moment?

This room was a bedroom, though not your usual bedroom, more of a 1920s showcase and a window into the past.

The enormous four-poster bed was austere in maroon and gold covers, softened by a mound of cushions. A dressing-table shone with polish and several mirrors and a tapestry-seated chest gleamed in the corner.

This wasn't happening. If he kissed her in here she'd

be gone. She looked up at him and felt like a rabbit caught in headlights.

Fergus paused at the panic in her face as he crossed the room and hesitated. He stopped and almost in slow motion he pulled her gently in front of him until her back was firm against his chest.

'Perhaps just a little experiment,' he said, and then turned them both towards the mirror so she could see their reflections in the glass.

Her body was framed by his, her spine rigid and unbending against him, and her eyes and mouth were narrow with wariness.

She saw his intention in his eyes in the mirror and she realised the kiss was as inevitable as his hand turning her body to face him.

She stood there, captive, and his beautiful eyes darkened to black and melted her resistance with barely any effort.

When his lips descended her eyelashes fluttered closed and she could do nothing but savour the homecoming of his mouth against her own.

His lips were softness and warmth giving way to the slow build-up of heat and firmness, growing more demanding and finally plundering until her hands clutched at his neck, seeking purchase in the storm, and then she demanded right back.

A slaking, satisfying, quenching kiss that she hadn't realised she'd needed but couldn't get enough of, and his arms held her safely away from the intrusion of the world into this timeless interlude her body needed but her brain denied.

Finally, a few minutes or many minutes later, achingly slowly, he drew away and his hands held her shoulders until her legs regained their strength.

She opened her eyes as he turned them to face the mirror again and a different woman stood there.

This woman was flushed, her languorous eyes complemented red swollen lips and she leant back against him for much-needed support.

Breathless and disorientated, her breasts ached and the fire in her belly throbbed in time to her heartbeat. She shook her head to deny he could do all that with one kiss.

He lifted her hand and kissed the inside of her wrist before gently leading her across the room. 'That explains a lot of things, I think. Perhaps we'd better move on. This way.'

He walked past the bed and opened another door. 'You can freshen up in here. I'll meet you in the library when you're ready.'

Ailee nodded, still stunned and with the tiniest gleam of something else. Frustration? Disappointment?

She heard him leave and she sank down onto a stool in the ornate bathroom, rested her head back against the cold tiled wall and closed her eyes.

Ailee felt as if she'd climbed a cliff rather than a flight of stairs. She wondered if he'd known it was going to be like that, how long he'd planned to do that, and if he was amused or…as frustrated as she was.

Whatever. She needed to explain her reasons, tell him about William, make Fergus realise he had to walk away before they got in any deeper, until she was free to live her own life.

Crack. There was a sound similar to one William had made many times over the years and, puzzled, she looked up. It couldn't have been. It had sounded like a ball had hit the wall. Who'd be playing cricket in the house?

Fergus rubbed his palm. He looked ruefully at the impervious wood on the wall and the pinkness on his fingers.

Not something he'd done for many years. At least he hadn't been stupid enough to punch it.

To walk away from Ailee in that room had been one of the hardest things Fergus had ever done. That moment in the car had shown him how easily she could send him to boiling point just by a teasing comment and tossing her hair.

The way she made him feel was something he'd never experienced, never believed was in him, a dangerousness and recklessness that belonged to someone else.

When she'd turned to look at him in front of the bed he hadn't been able to stop himself. It hadn't been his original intention but he'd had to take that final step and pull her into his arms.

This was out of control and he should never have brought her here.

A few minutes later Ailee entered the library and she avoided his eyes. Instead, she looked at the portrait above the mantelpiece that dominated the room.

'My mother,' Fergus said, but Ailee didn't need to be told that.

The woman was tall, judging by the rail on the staircase she was standing beside. Her hair, the same chocolate brown colour as Fergus's, was coiled in a knot at her neck and the dark bedroom eyes were eerily similar to the ones Ailee had had no defence against barely ten minutes ago.

'She was a beautiful woman.'

Fergus nodded. 'Sophie takes after her.'

Ailee half smiled. 'So does her son.'

She looked away from the compelling portrait and raised her chin. 'You shouldn't have brought me here, Fergus.'

'That's the first time you've called me Fergus since you left my bed.'

After what had happened upstairs she'd known it was on his mind but she hadn't expected him to be so brazen about it. His words struck low in her stomach and she sucked in her breath. 'Don't.'

'Don't what?' He narrowed his eyes like a hunter sensing prey, and she felt trapped by his strength and her own weakness.

She turned her back on him and walked to the window that looked out over the lawn. 'Don't remind me. Singapore was a mistake and I need to explain something.'

He ignored the latter half of her sentence and concentrated on one word. 'And what just happened or nearly happened upstairs—was that a mistake, too?'

He raised his eyebrows, daring her to dispute it. 'I've never felt anything less like a mistake. We connected. The same happened in Singapore and then you left. With that ridiculous note, as if we'd shared a cup of tea.'

She glanced back at him and the sombre note in his voice made her frown.

He stroked the lid of the steaming pot Martha had left and then crossed the room to stand beside her shoulder, not touching, as if he couldn't trust himself, but close enough for her to feel his heat.

She turned her face away and he went on.

'Why did you leave like that? You agreed we should see each other in Sydney. I didn't dream that connection, Ailee. Did I?' He lifted her chin with his finger and she was forced to look at him.

This was a disaster. She should never have come. This was one hundred per cent his battleground and she needed to get out of there.

'Yes, there was a connection, but I need air. Take me outside. I need to explain but I can't breathe in here.'

Because you're larger than life in this room and I feel intimidated by my weakness when I'm alone with you. And I'm frightened what will happen if you kiss me again. You could make me do things I'd never dream of doing, would go against my own soul. She didn't say it out loud—it was bad enough, admitting it to herself.

'All right, we'll go outside, but I want some answers.'

He led the way to a side door that led into a conservatory furnished with white cane furniture and dozens of lush green potted plants. In another time and place she would have loved this room. The windows were full-length French doors and he opened one to allow her to precede him onto the tiled balcony.

She drew a deep breath at the fresh air and the space

she'd created between them and headed for the stone steps that connected the balcony to the lawn.

Fergus was determined as he caught up with her on the grass and swung her around. 'When you left like that I assumed you didn't care. Was I wrong? If you tell me you didn't feel the same, I'll leave you alone and never speak of it again.' His eyes bored into hers and then narrowed as she hesitated.

It would be so easy. Just lie and say he meant nothing to her. Ailee opened her mouth and then closed it again. She had to be honest with him.

'You are right. There is something between us.' She paused. 'But…' She felt him stiffen beside her.

She went on doggedly, 'The time of our meeting couldn't have been worse. I can't look ahead that way. What I see in you is something I've waited to find for a long time but Singapore wasn't the time…' He didn't let her finish.

Fergus shook his head. 'What about now? You have the world to offer me. I know I'm moving fast, hell, we both move faster than light when we're together, but I can't let you get away now that I've found you.'

He was right beside her now and slid his hand possessively over the curve of her shoulder until her skin glowed with heat from his hand.

She was fine as long as he didn't touch her, but as soon as his skin met hers she weakened like a child against him. She could feel her knees tremble and she stepped away from his contact before it was too late. His hand fell to his side and she bit her lip.

'You tremble when I touch you and you run if I don't

stop you from doing so.' His face twisted into a cynical smile. 'What do you think that means?'

His words settled between them and she was too frightened of their power to pick them up.

'We barely know each other.'

He actually laughed out loud but the sound was anything but amusing. 'We know each other intimately.'

Silence fell between them as they both contemplated that statement and the pictures filled Ailee's memories and paralysed her. Then he went on.

'I've seen too much of life not to know my mind. I thought about how complicated you were going to make my world the first time I saw you.'

She felt the tears stinging at the backs of her eyes and she blinked them away. This was too important.

'That's exactly why this is such poor timing. I don't need this pressure. There is so much going on in my life at this moment. You and your daughter don't need someone you can't trust to be there in your life.'

He looked at her and for the first time she felt he really listened.

'Not be there in what way?' His words drifted between them like a cool breeze, zephyr-like and soft. 'And we'll leave my daughter out of this.'

'Your daughter is part of the reason.'

And then Sophie was there. The dark-haired young girl dressed in a martial arts kit ran across the lawn to meet them. 'Daddy? I'm home. Who's your friend?'

CHAPTER SEVEN

SOPHIE MCVICKER was a miniature of the woman in the portrait and obviously another determined lady. Ailee wondered in which ways Sophie would reflect the maternal side of her family.

Fergus turned slowly and faced his daughter. 'Hello, Sophie. What happened to martial arts?'

'Chrissy Smythe fell and broke her wrist and Mr Ting had to go with her to the hospital so we finished early.'

Fergus nodded. 'Poor Chrissy.' He turned to Ailee. 'Dr Ailee Green, meet my daughter, Sophie.'

Ailee held out her hand and shook the girl's fingers, which flopped like a wilted flower. Sophie was playing droopy princess, and Ailee tried to contain the twitch of her lips. It was a struggle.

When Ailee had been a teenager, people who'd shaken hands like that had been called fish.

Sophie looked Ailee up and down as they held hands. 'You're very tall, aren't you? I'm going to be tall like my father and grandmother.'

Ailee smiled. 'Yes, I can see that. But you shake hands like a fish.'

The young girl blinked, stared, tightened her grip and shook hands properly. Slowly they smiled at each other.

Fergus watched with interest as Sophie dropped all pretence at aloofness. He wished his daughter would drop it with him.

'Do you work with my dad at the new hospital?'

Ailee nodded. 'I'm one of the transplant co-ordinators at the moment so I don't go into surgery.'

'Can you do operations?'

Ailee nodded. 'I've just finished three months in Scotland with a professor in renal surgery.'

Fergus stared at her. 'Professor Giles? At the Edinburgh Infirmary?'

'And Ian Forrest. But enough of me. I'd really like a cup of tea and one of those gorgeous-looking cakes that Martha has waiting in the library.'

Sophie clapped her hand over her mouth. 'I was supposed to remind you of that. We'd better go in.'

They all turned and headed for the house and Ailee was quite surprised how far they'd walked. Probably because she'd been walking quickly to escape the impending disclosures that she still hadn't made. Now his daughter was involved.

Fergus was quiet and she knew there were some big questions coming her way soon.

There was no chance for Fergus to ask anything because his daughter monopolised Ailee's attention as if she were starved of female conversation. Sophie could talk while she poured, though, and Ailee was very impressed with her hostess skills.

'So who do you think has the best dress sense?' Sophie

held out a magazine with two glamorous young women on the cover as a plate of dainty cakes changed hands.

Ailee looked at Fergus for help and he was watching with a small smile on his face. 'Um—they're singers,' he clarified, obviously trying hard to stay up to scratch with his daughter's favourites.

'Definitely her.' Ailee didn't know the other one but she'd look out for her. She took a bite and the morsel melted in her mouth.

Sophie was too busy talking to eat. 'Do you ski? My father promised me a holiday skiing but then chose to work during his holidays.' She pouted.

Ailee glanced at Fergus, who said nothing in his own defence. 'I know three young people whose lives have been changed because your dad came when our hospital needed him. One of them could have died if we hadn't found a replacement surgeon.' She softened her words with a smile. 'It is disappointing for you, though.'

Sophie looked at her father. 'I have compensation coming my way and I'd really like to go to New Zealand in the winter. Unfortunately he hates planes.'

Ailee remembered that Fergus hated planes. Those memories made her remember other things. Luckily Sophie prattled on.

'They say it's even better than Thredbo.'

Ailee was having trouble keeping up because every subject seemed to bring back more memories that she'd locked away from that time with Fergus. 'I'm a tobogganer, sorry. Haven't tried skiing but I have been to New Zealand and it is lovely.'

'I was a boarder at school but Dad said he missed me

too much so I came home. I don't believe him but I like being a day student better.'

Fergus met Ailee's look and tilted his head in acknowledgment. She was glad he'd decided to bring his daughter home. Sophie seemed a bright young woman, if a little hard on Fergus.

Sophie looked up at Ailee after handing her father his cup and saucer. 'Are you staying for dinner?'

'No.' Ailee put down her empty plate. 'I have to go home. I promised my mother I'd be home for a family dinner, which I hope I can still eat, and it's getting late.'

Sophie hadn't taken her eyes off Ailee. 'Will you come again?'

'We'll see. But it has been lovely to meet you, Sophie.' Ailee held out her hand, sure that this time the grip would be firm.

Sophie ignored her hand, hugged Ailee, and then kissed her cheek.

'I liked meeting you, too. Dad never brings women home.'

'I'm honoured.' Ailee looked at Fergus and dreaded the trip home. Suddenly she couldn't face the whole explanation scene and her nerves were shattered. 'Would you like me to order a taxi, Fergus? It would save you going out again.'

'I'll take you home.' There was no doubt that Fergus had earmarked the return journey for some information-sharing and Ailee was trapped.

'Can I come?' Sophie's request hung in the air and Ailee avoided Fergus as she looked at his daughter.

'I don't mind, but it's up to your father.'

Sophie didn't look at Fergus either. 'The only problem is I get sick in the back.'

Ailee was quick to offer. 'I'll sit in the back, and you can sit with your father in the front.'

'No, you won't.' Fergus said it mildly enough but both women knew there was no choice.

Now Sophie looked at her father. 'I could probably sit in the back for a short trip,' she suggested, and as they moved towards the door she whispered to Ailee, 'You wanted me to come, didn't you?'

'Thanks,' Ailee said, and Sophie gave a satisfied nod.

The car journey was quite strained and when Fergus opened her door back at the hospital, his words brushed her neck as she walked past.

'We're not finished. I'll ring you.' Then he helped his daughter into the front and walked back to his own door.

'Thank you for the tea and cakes,' Ailee said.

There was humour in the look Fergus gave her. 'It was an interesting evening. I'll speak to you soon.'

Fergus watched her in the rear-view mirror as he drove away, noting she didn't turn around to wave. He'd never been so unsure about someone else's feelings in his life. She sent out such mixed signals it was a wonder his head wasn't spinning.

He guaranteed he reached her when he kissed her, but the rest of the time he was in the dark. Was he crazy to lay his heart on the block again for her to slice up into little pieces, like she had in Singapore?

As he drove he mulled over the way Ailee had behaved that afternoon, and he came to the conclusion that there was hope.

So what were Ailee's reasons for not wanting a relationship?

He decided she probably had a tortured past and had been hurt by some man. He could deal with that. These were all things he'd never thought to have to consider again when Stella had died.

He admitted to himself that he was back where he'd been in Singapore when he'd begun to know her.

Thinking long term and even beyond to life and marriage. To his intense surprise he wasn't fazed by any of those concepts—only that the plan could fail if Ailee continued to oppose his suit.

If it all came to nothing, there would be some personal cost.

But he was willing to take that risk. He had to be careful for Sophie, though.

'You like her, don't you, Dad?'

He'd thought Sophie had been listening to her MP3 player, which travelled everywhere with her. He glanced across at her. The expression on her face reminded him of her mother when she'd been indulgent of his 'man's' ways.

The usual pain from his loss of Stella didn't come as viciously as it once had and he was thankful for that.

He smiled at the tiny warming from his daughter. It was unusual for Sophie to initiate a conversation.

'Yes, I do, Sophie. Do you like Ailee?' He slowed the car as he looked across at his daughter again.

'I think she's neat and I think she's kind, too. Elizabeth Arrow's step mother is a witch. I don't think Ailee would be a witch. It would be good for you to have another woman around for a change. You might stay home more—especially if she has a baby.'

Fergus nearly ran into the gate as he drove into his driveway. His daughter was way ahead of him.

'I might need to get to know Ailee better before we think about babies. And I'd really prefer if you didn't mention this conversation to anyone at school. OK?'

'Sure, Dad.'

His daughter was twelve going on twenty and it was darned scary.

Ailee heard the car pull away and forced herself not to turn around. She drew in a shuddering sigh and wished she'd had the chance to tell him. The longer she left it the bigger her secret loomed, which was ridiculous. Of all the people in the world to understand, Fergus should.

Still, she needed to think through the implications of the last hour and be fair to both of them. Actually, the three of them.

At least she had the weekend to get it right before Monday.

Ailee glanced at her watch and her eyes widened. She had only enough time to jump in her car and make it home before her mother's roast was ruined.

'So how was work?' William appeared quite chirpy at the dinner table. He'd only just come in from being out with some friends and looked different to his usual solemn self.

'Work was fine.' Ailee glanced at his plate. 'And since when do you eat bananas?'

Ailee raised her eyebrows at the tiny half-banana William had tucked under his plate and, caught out, her brother shrugged.

'It's my once-a-month treat, and I'm having dialysis tomorrow.'

William knew he had to be careful of foods that contained 'dangerous salts' like potassium, and his fluid restrictions were the part he hated the most—he was allowed to drink less than a litre of fluid a day.

When he was well enough, he went out with his friends on Friday nights. He couldn't drink alcohol, mainly because of the fluid amounts involved and the chemicals his body couldn't get rid of.

Like most dialysis patients, William had established a good rapport with the staff and mostly older patients who came into the dialysis clinic at the hospital on the same days as he did.

Unlike less fortunate end-stage kidney-disease sufferers, William knew it was ending soon. He was guaranteed a kidney. Ailee's kidney!

Ailee smiled across at her brother. 'You're looking stronger.'

'I'm getting there. The next assessment clinic will be the big test and it's not far off. I'm pretty nervous about that.'

'I've got my fingers crossed.'

Helen looked across at her son because she knew how much depended on it. 'William said the man standing in for Mr Harry seems very good. Do you think he'll be the one who does the surgery if it all goes ahead quickly?'

Ailee hadn't considered that. It was a disquieting

thought and she wasn't so sure Fergus would be happy either when he found out who the donor was. She concentrated on her mother's question to avoid thinking about Fergus operating on her.

'Fergus McVicker has been seconded from Sydney West. It all depends on Mrs Harry and how quickly she recovers from her stroke whether Mr McVicker stays on for two or four weeks.'

Her mother still looked worried at the change of surgeon at this late stage so Ailee went on when the last thing she wanted to do was talk about Fergus. 'He's dedicated and apparently a whiz in Theatre. It seems that he's the best laparoscopic surgeon in Australia.'

'Then William can't lose, whoever the surgeon is. We need the best when my only two children depend on the man.' Helen put her napkin to her lips and closed her eyes.

Then she smiled tremulously and stood up. 'I'll just get some more vegetables,' she said brightly, and left the table.

William and Ailee looked at each other and Ailee stood up. They both knew their mother would be crying in the kitchen and Ailee patted her brother's shoulder as she followed her mother.

Helen wiped her eyes as her daughter came in.

'We will be fine,' Ailee said.

'I know. I'm being a drama queen.'

Ailee smiled and dropped a kiss on her mother's cheek. 'No, you're not. You're being a wonderful, caring mother and we wouldn't have you any other way.'

Later that evening, Ailee searched out William after her mother had gone to bed. She leaned over his chair and ruffled his hair. 'Hey, Will. How's it going?'

William smiled crookedly up at her and shrugged. 'The usual.'

Ailee sat down next to him. 'Do you mind if I ask you something?'

'Shoot.'

'How are you coping with dialysis? I know you hate it and I know you don't have much choice, but it must be hard, especially when you're going through a rough patch like the last couple of weeks.'

William looked away. 'Dialysis sucks but death is worse. I guess that keeps me going.'

Such basic equations from an eighteen-year-old made Ailee wince.

He shrugged and flicked the pages of the television guide. Ailee thanked God that her brother still felt it was worth it.

After talking to Lawrence—had it only been today?—she'd been worried William was becoming morbid, too. She'd noticed a few deviations from his usual happy self and even wondered if they'd lost a little closeness since she'd come home.

William went on. 'Dialysis gives a rotten quality of life—three days a week at least tied to a machine for half the day. Watching everything you eat. Can't go out with my mates and have a few drinks. This horrible fistula...' he shook his wrist where his veins stood out, scarred and bulging where a grafted artery had strengthened his vein for needle access to his bloodstream '...would scare any self-respecting girl away. They'd probably think I'm a drug addict anyway because of the needle marks up my arm.'

He shrugged. 'The day before I go for dialysis I feel sick because my blood's filling up with toxins. The day after treatment I need to recover from the strain of the procedure and the cramps 'cos they have to take extra fluid off. I can't remember when I last felt really well.'

He sniffed. 'They tell me all that will change after the op but the drug regime to stop your kidney being rejected seems pretty heavy. I'm not hanging out for that either.'

Ailee nodded. 'We're here for you. I think you're incredibly brave.'

He shrugged and then looked away. 'We all know you're the brave one.'

For a moment Ailee thought there was a bitter note to her brother's voice but then he smiled up at her and she pushed the feeling away.

On Saturday morning Ailee woke in her lonely bed, and as her dreams faded she thought of Fergus and the way he'd kissed her yesterday.

She could almost feel his arms around her, the warmth of him and the way she'd looked with his hands holding her body, and she wanted those things again.

But if she wanted those things, she would have to include him in her plans, and her reasons for not doing so were still there.

Ailee rolled over and pulled the pillow over her head to block out the bright light.

She'd slept late because it had taken her so long to get to sleep.

The phone started ringing and Ailee scrambled out of bed to get it before it stopped. It wouldn't be for her because she wasn't on call as co-ordinator and William seemed to get the most calls anyway.

'Ailee?' She recognised Fergus's voice immediately and her grip tightened on the receiver.

CHAPTER EIGHT

AILEE glanced around but no one was in earshot. 'Yes?'

'How are you?' There was amusement in Fergus's voice and she couldn't help the curve of her own lips.

'Fine.' Where was this going?

'Are you up to visiting us again? My daughter requests the pleasure of your company and she's been talking to me more than she has for a long time.'

She needed to get less involved with Fergus's daughter, not more involved. 'I'm not sure this is a good idea.'

'Would you do this, just today, for me, please?'

It was hard to say no. Ailee stalled. 'What did you have in mind?'

'Sophie likes tennis and we have a court here. I suggested she have some friends around and she asked if you would come, too. Any chance?'

'I'm not very good.' It was a lame excuse and nowhere near the definite no she'd meant to say.

'There's three other pre-adolescent females coming. I'll be outnumbered. Help.'

'I'm sure you'll manage.'

'Just this once. How about I pick you up in an hour?'

He was railroading her again. 'You don't know where I live.'

'My next question.'

'No. I'll drive myself.' And then I can bring myself home when I want to, she thought. Especially if I get a chance to tell him about William, I might need to leave.

There was a small pause until he answered. 'See you soon, then.'

Ailee put the phone down slowly and straightened up.

'Who was that, darling?' Helen was on her way to the kitchen.

'Someone from work, inviting me for a game of tennis.'

'I hope you said yes.'

Ailee looked at her mother and then she laughed. 'Yes, Mother. I will go out and play.'

Helen smiled sheepishly. 'Well, you haven't left our sides except to go to work. You need to have your own life, especially while you are well.'

Ailee hugged her mother. 'I'll be well again after this operation, too, so stop worrying.'

When she arrived at the McVicker house there was a red sports car and a long saloon parked outside the front door. Two curvy blonde women sailed down the front stairs past Ailee and shook their heads.

'Better him than us,' one of them said. She looked Ailee up and down and then smiled. 'If you're looking for a wild time, it's happening in there.'

Ailee smiled bemusedly at the women and climbed

the stairs. A slightly fazed Martha opened the door and ushered her in warmly.

'Now, you might be able to sort this, Dr Green. I fear Fergus is out of his depth.'

Loud music was coming from the library and Ailee searched her mind for the memory of a stereo. She couldn't remember one in the book-lined room.

She walked across and opened the library door, and the music assaulted her ears, along with the visual impact of four short-skirted pre-teens in crop tops and tennis shoes gyrating.

At first she couldn't see Fergus but then spotted him peering at the ghetto-blaster, obviously searching for the volume control.

Sophie grinned and waved as Ailee dodged past the dancers with a little gyration of her own until she came up behind Fergus.

'It's here,' Ailee shouted, but it was her finger, not her voice, that drew his attention, and she slid the volume control down to barely painful.

As she did so, she turned to catch Sophie's eye and tapped her ears to explain the change in volume. Sophie shrugged and nodded but seemed happy enough.

Ailee pointed to the connecting door to the observatory and Fergus agreed with fervour.

The door shut out almost half of the sound but wasn't enough for him. He took Ailee's hand and steered her through to the outside terrace, and when that door was shut as well it was almost peaceful in the warm outside air.

'Good grief. Thank you for coming.' He gestured to

a white wrought-iron table and chairs and waited until she was seated under the shade of an open umbrella before he sat down.

Martha appeared as if by magic with orange juice and ice cubes in tall glasses for them and a jug and smaller glasses for the invaders when they came.

'Much more sensible outside, I agree, Dr Green.'

'Please, call me Ailee, Martha, and thank you for this.' She gestured to her glass.

'I see it's a little quieter now,' Martha teased Fergus. He took it good-naturedly as his housekeeper left them.

Ailee laughed. 'You shouldn't have bought Sophie a portable sound system.'

Fergus held up his hands and waved then. 'Not my fault. One of the little darlings brought it with her this morning.'

'What an enterprising female. Why so deafening?'

'Apparently that was Sophie's all-time favourite song and it needs to be at decibel ten to be really appreciated.'

'You exaggerate, but it was loud.'

His admiring gaze ran over her T-shirt and micro shorts then back to her face. 'You look gorgeous.'

'Thank you, kind sir. I don't own a tennis skirt. You don't look bad yourself.' Fergus lounged in cargo shorts and an open-necked white shirt and they smiled at each other like idiots in mutual admiration.

The peace was shattered as the girls poured through the conservatory door and circled their table.

'Hello, Ailee.' Sophie grinned. 'Have you come to save Dad from us?'

'Yep. So who have we here?'

'Dianne, Prue and Angela.' Sophie pointed out each girl—one with braces, one with bright red nail polish and one with the sweetest face and smile.

Mentally Ailee dubbed them dentist, polish and angel so that she would remember their names.

'Dianne, Prue and Angela.' The names matched the prompts and she had them in her memory now. 'How do you do?'

After refreshments they all trooped towards the tennis court and Fergus watched his daughter hang back to walk with Ailee.

Sophie looked shy for a second, which wasn't like her and made him realise how important Ailee's presence was. He hoped he was doing the right thing by encouraging this friendship.

'Thanks for coming, Ailee,' Sophie said.

'Thank you for the invitation.' She glanced conspiratorially at the young girl. 'I wouldn't have missed your father with his hands over his ears. All we need to do now is beat him at tennis and I can go home happy.'

Sophie glanced across at her father with a smile and Fergus savoured the laughter on both their faces and the fact that he was included in his daughter's warmth.

'I may give you a run for your money,' he said mildly as he put the racket bag he was carrying down on the bench beside the court.

'You girls have a game first and we'll watch and then Ailee and I will play the losers in a knockout.'

The morning passed with much hilarity, especially when Ailee teased Fergus about his poor level of play.

They'd swapped the teams around several times and Ailee and Sophie were playing against Fergus and Prue.

'We win,' Ailee crowed, as they met at the net to shake hands. She laughed up at Fergus and he grinned down at her.

'Will we tell her?' Fergus asked his daughter.

Sophie giggled. 'Dad's been playing with his left hand all morning and he's right-handed.'

'That's terrible. Here I was thinking I wasn't too bad at all. I won't have it. Play with your right hand and don't hold back, Fergus McVicker.'

One more game later, Ailee and Sophie walked off without having scored a point and now the other girls wanted to play Fergus with his right hand.

Sophie and Ailee sat down beside one of Martha's jugs of iced orange and Ailee pretended to be offended.

'He's too good.'

Sophie looked across at her father, who had easily lobbed a shot back to the far corner of the court to have his opponents scrambling. 'He's been hilarious today. My friends said he was a crack-up.' She looked a little surprised to be proud of him.

'His sense of humour is a wonderful part of him. Along with his rotten left-handed tennis skills.'

Sophie smiled and then her face became more serious. 'We haven't used the court together since my mother died.'

'You should play together more often. I know he misses being your friend.' She tested Sophie's reaction to talking about Stella's death. 'Your father said it was a shock to everyone when your mother had complications after surgery.'

Sophie stared across the grass. 'It should never have happened. How can a doctor not be able to save his own wife? How could Dad let it happen?'

Ailee slipped her arms around Sophie's shoulders and hugged her before sitting back. 'Anger is a part of grief. Your dad is a very talented surgeon but I guess they wouldn't have let him anywhere near your mother because surgeons aren't allowed to operate on or look after their own family.'

Sophie looked at Ailee. 'Has anyone died while you were operating?'

'No, but sometimes I've had to operate on people who have just died so they can donate their organs to others.'

Sophie shook her head as if to ward off the mental picture. 'I don't want to think about that or that part of my dad's work.'

Ailee raised her eyebrows. 'OK. But it's a big part and he's one of the leaders in Australia.' Ailee filled both their glasses with more juice.

'So tell me about when you boarded at school. Is it better as a day student now?'

'Heaps better. Actually...' she looked across at her father '...I think it made me appreciate Dad more. I missed him when I stayed away all week even though he's not here much.'

Ailee smiled. 'I think he missed you, too.'

'He must have.' Sophie glanced across at her father, who was shaking hands at the net with her friends. 'He asked if I'd rather come home again.'

The others joined them.

Fergus poured himself a glass of juice and raised it

to his daughter. 'You played really well, Sophie. I'm most impressed.' Sophie glowed with the praise and Fergus put the empty glass down and rubbed her back with affection. Ailee was pleased to see Sophie lean back into her father and smile up at him. Things were definitely getting better there.

Fergus met Ailee's eyes over the top of his daughter's dark hair and he looked content. Any positive results for Fergus's relationship with his daughter made her visit worthwhile. Ailee smiled back at him. But she should go and let them have some time together. There wasn't going to be an opportunity to discuss William today.

'Let's go up and have lunch.' Fergus rounded up the rackets and repacked the bag, and Ailee collected the glasses.

They all carried glasses and jugs and trooped up to the house where Martha had sandwiches and savoury pies ready to serve.

The other girls left soon after lunch and Ailee glanced at her watch.

'I might head off, too.'

Fergus looked up with a frown and Sophie pouted.

Ailee smiled at Sophie. 'Have some time with your dad. He doesn't get you to himself very much and you have all afternoon. I have to do some things at home.'

'Will you come back another time?'

'Absolutely.' She pretended to scowl at Fergus. 'Right after I have tennis lessons.'

But any future visits had to wait because the chance of Sophie becoming distressed about Ailee's operation was becoming more likely the more she saw of the young girl. Sophie was crying out for a female role model and at this point in time Ailee felt she was being dishonest with her.

Sophie laughed at the tennis reference and they walked Ailee out to her car. Sophie hugged Ailee and Ailee encircled the young girl's slim form and hugged her back. 'Thanks for asking me, Sophie.'

Sophie smiled up at her. 'I thought Dad might need adult reinforcements.' She glanced at her father and then Ailee and turned to leave. 'I'll leave you two to say goodbye.'

'Thank you, Sophie.' Fergus raised his eyebrows at Ailee and waited until his daughter was out of sight.

'So when do we have this talk, Ailee Green?'

'Soon.'

'Early tomorrow morning?'

'I run in the mornings.'

'Ah, yes. I remember. Along Balmoral beach.'

On Sunday morning, Ailee woke to a feeling of decision. The next time she saw Fergus she would explain about William and discuss if and why she needed to distance herself from Sophie, at least until after the operation.

Her heart pounded and suddenly the weight of the bedclothes on her chest was too heavy. She threw the covers off and sat up. She needed to get out of there because she couldn't sit still until it was done.

Dressed and with her hair tied back, the cold air struck her face as she opened the front door and turned her joggers along the path towards the beach. She needed to be as healthy as possible before the operation to help her get over it more quickly.

The scar from the nephrectomy would go a third of the way around her body and she would be doing little exercise for the next few weeks. She tried to eat healthy foods and prepare herself to be in optimum fitness for the coming operation.

She'd been warned that the operation site pain would be considerable but there would be medication she could take for that, although if Fergus performed the operation, the keyhole method was apparently less traumatic and shortened the recovery time.

Dr Harry was old-fashioned and was the expert on open excisions. He believed there was less trauma to the donated kidney via the open method and Ailee was happy for William to have her kidney in the best condition it could be in.

The sun rose above the horizon and shone into her eyes. It was earlier than she usually ran and there were not many other runners up, which seemed unusual for the paths around Balmoral.

Ahead, a lone figure sat on a bench overlooking the beach and there was something about the set of his shoulders that reminded her of Fergus.

Ailee's heart began to pound and as she drew level she saw she hadn't been mistaken. Her feet slowed and she came to a stop beside him.

'Fergus,' she said, and he turned to look at her.

'Ailee. Well met.' His glance warmed her already pink cheeks. He looked strong and fit but there were lines of fatigue under his eyes and her heart contracted.

Had she done this to him? He was a good man and didn't deserve being messed about.

'You're walking early. Why's that?' She thought she knew.

'For walking? I couldn't sleep. For ending up here? Someone I know lives around here and she told me she ran on this beach.'

'Come back for breakfast and then I'll run you home,' she offered, not sure what she would tell her mother.

He smiled ruefully. 'Do I look that worn out?'

Ailee pretended to consider. 'Put it this way—I don't think you'll enjoy the walk home.'

'How about we have a coffee here on the beach?' He pointed to the vendor setting up his stall.

'So much for my run,' Ailee complained, but she knew which she'd rather do and there were things she'd been waiting to say. She paused for him to stand and they crossed the street together.

When they were seated back on the bench with their polystyrene cups, neither seemed eager to start the conversation.

Ailee practised her opening sentence to explain about William. It was the right thing to do. When he knew about her brother, she'd leave the decision to him.

'I'm sorry I kissed you on Friday,' he said.

Ailee's train of thought derailed. That wasn't what she'd expected him to say. 'Why is that?' She looked at him.

He didn't say anything for a moment and, in fact, he really didn't have to say a word. The searing look he gave her made his words superfluous. 'Because I haven't slept since then and I want to do more than kiss you right now.'

He leant towards her and she found herself drawn closer as if pulled by an unseen force, but the moment was lost in a screech of tyres that shattered the peace of the beach on the road behind them. Two horns blared at each other before the cars roared off in different directions.

Ailee and Fergus both winced and sighed with relief at the lack of impact, more aware than a lot of people about the fragility of life.

Ailee looked back at him. This was crazy. Fergus could melt her with one look and they were dancing around the attraction as if they had all the time in the world to choose to fall in love.

'I'm not sorry you kissed me.'

'Oh, really?' His mouth lifted and the glint of humour made her lips twitch.

'Yep, but we have to talk.' She did care for him but there were obstacles. She wasn't backing away this time.

His hand reached across the bench and lifted her fingers and turned them over palm-up. 'Fine. But let's do it somewhere more private. Sophie went off last night to sleep at Prue's house and won't be home until after lunch.'

He pulled her closer along the bench until her hip rested against his. 'Come home with me for a while.'

Her lips twitched. 'Are you propositioning me, Mr McVicker?'

He raised one eyebrow. 'My word, I am.' When he lifted her hand to his lips, she closed her eyes briefly just to feel it all.

He kissed her hand softly, warm and tingling in the centre of her palm, and the sensation travelled straight to her stomach where it glowed like a single hot coal that had lain dormant since Singapore.

His voice dropped and seemed to brush against her skin. 'Why have we danced around this so long?'

She shook her head, without an answer.

Suddenly it was tragic. She sighed. 'There are things you don't know about me.'

He shook his head. 'Whatever I don't know can't change the feelings that I have for you.'

She still wasn't sure she had the right to intrude, and grow larger, in his and his daughter's lives with so much indecision hanging over her. They would talk about that and she could hardly wait.

In unison they dropped their unfinished drinks into the waste bin and he squeezed her hand as they turned towards her house.

Her mother had dropped William at dialysis, and when Ailee ran in to collect her car keys there was no one to see her flushed cheeks. She dashed off a quick note to say she'd be home around lunchtime.

As they drove towards Mosman, Ailee could feel the warmth of his gaze, and when she glanced across he smiled and rested his hand on her leg. It all felt so right. She looked down at his fingers curved around her thigh and grinned. 'Nobody has held my leg since high school.'

'I'd like to do a lot more but I'm playing it safe while you drive.'

'That seems a sensible idea.' She felt like laughing

out loud just because she was with him and suddenly the day was brighter and more exciting than any before.

He squeezed her leg briefly and then took his hand away. 'But incredibly difficult to stick to.'

The tension mounted as they drove in through the gates and this time Fergus took her hand and led her around the back of the house and in through an enormous kitchen with a black slate floor.

Ailee followed, glad they didn't see anyone because Fergus took her straight up to his room with no pretence of conversation. Her heart pounded and her mouth dried.

Fergus towed her into a bedroom similar in size to the one she'd been in the other day, but this one was in greens and blues and looked a little more lived-in.

They stopped in the middle of the room and he captured her other hand so that she swung around and faced him.

He stared down into her eyes. 'I know we have to talk. But after Friday I know it isn't going to change anything. So can you wait?'

She shook her head in denial but her body leaned into him.

Fergus smiled. 'Should I ask you again?'

Ailee leaned up and brushed his mouth with hers before nodding.

Already her knees felt weak at his intention, and when his mouth came down Ailee sighed into him. Homecoming. That's what it was like and it was what she'd woken this morning and needed.

It seemed that Fergus needed it, too.

His strength and gentleness created havoc as he

slipped her top from her shoulders and left her breasts bare to the coolness in the room.

She needed to feel his skin under her hands and she peeled the shirt from his shoulders. With a final flurry of discarded clothes he pulled her back onto the bed in his arms and rolled on top of her to stare down at her. His gaze swept over her like a blast of heat and she followed his glance down the length of their bodies.

His legs lay on either side of hers as he held his weight off her body, his well-defined biceps and glorious chest so strongly beautiful he took her breath away.

Then he rolled and took her with him to lie on their sides facing each other, and this time when he kissed her there were no other thoughts except the taste and feel of Fergus's mouth on hers. The hunger between them exploded and expanded and she was carried with him into a surging maelstrom that left them both tossed and breathless.

When he finally lifted his lips from hers her eyes were too heavy to open and she arched her neck as he descended her body to pay homage with his hands and mouth until she ached to be possessed.

He paused briefly to protect her before again he knelt above her, and this time she lifted herself towards him.

She opened her eyes as he entered her. She knew this man, this recent stranger, like she knew herself, and she gloried in his possession because he was her destiny. If not now, then some time that had to come in the future.

His possession deepened until her eyes widened further and he stopped, filling her, incredibly hard and hot and what she needed so badly that she wrapped her legs around him and clutched at his back with her fingers.

He buried his face in her hair for a moment and she could feel the heat of his breath on her neck. They stayed at that point for what seemed a lifetime. Then he lifted above her to withdraw.

She felt the breath leave her body as he did. She was weak and yet aching for his return and then the surge of his homecoming rushed the heat to her face and she cried out as he filled her again.

Their rhythm burnt through her body in scalding waves and he murmured her name and whispered how beautiful she was, and the tempo increased, as did her moans and the tension in her fingers. She arched against him with all her strength, clenching with her inner muscles until she could bear it no longer.

Ailee heard his breath catch and then she seemed to shatter into a million tiny lights, pulsing as he shuddered against her, clutching her tightly against him as he followed her over the edge.

Afterwards they lay again on their sides, chests heaving, he still within her, staring at each other. He shook his head softly as he reached out and pulled the sheet over them.

Fergus was in shock. What had just happened? He felt like a survivor from a raging storm.

He'd loved his wife, had never been unfaithful, had never really expected to find love again. But this was no passing fancy.

What Ailee had done to him had touched him and he

hoped she felt the same because he would never forget this moment as long as he lived.

He tightened his hands on her shoulders and the thought of his recent possession made him stir again. Her eyes widened and she smiled cheekily at him as he gently began to move.

Afterwards they fell asleep in each other's arms and when they woke up it was lunchtime.

Fergus woke first and he wondered, as he lay on his side and watched this woman wake for the second time in his life, what lay ahead of them. He hoped many more years of watching her wake up. It was a big call but suddenly he was certain.

He grinned crookedly at her as she looked around at the room properly for the first time.

'The room is a little overdone, I know, but the bed is very comfortable,' Fergus said.

Ailee could tell it wasn't the furniture he'd enjoyed.

Enjoyed was too weak a word. She rolled onto her back and avoided his eyes. They'd penetrated each other's souls back there and their intimacy made her blush so deeply her hands came up to cover the heat in her cheeks.

'How on earth did we come to this point with each other so quickly? I can't believe I'm here with you.' She glanced down at the sheet covering her body. 'like this.'

'Neither can I,' he said huskily as he moved closer until his shoulder touched hers again. 'I haven't been alive like this for a very long time.' His gaze swept over her and tingled her skin with his look of possession.

Ailee wanted to believe him. His words fitted the moment perfectly and Fergus was everything she'd dreamed of in a lover and in a man. Gentle, yet powerful, and the way he worshipped her body made her feel as if she was the most beautiful woman in the world.

He kissed her and this time the fire was quick to sweep over them.

'I have so needed you against me,' he murmured as his lips burnt a trail down her neck and Ailee arched into him as his mouth closed over the peak of her breast. She dug her fingers into the strength of his shoulder blades and then down his back, remembering…

'You are so beautiful,' he sighed into the hollow between her breasts, and Ailee held his head and pulled him back towards her, so hungry to feel his mouth she was sure she would go insane if he didn't kiss her.

She slid under him until she was level with his face and found sanity there. Connected, their bodies reunited and the world receded.

Afterwards they lay on their sides again, staring at each other, and Fergus pulled the sheet up and over their heads so that they lay in their own world, holding hands in the white-out. The sun shone through the tree outside the window and dappled their tent as it billowed.

'OK,' he said softly. 'What do you need to tell me?'

Ailee looked at the man beside her, the strong planes of his face carved in relief by shadows, his beautiful mouth that could give so much heat, and his caring eyes that made tears spring to her own. Of course Fergus would understand and support her.

'It's about my brother.'

Fergus nodded.

Before she could say another word, the insistent tone of his pager sounded and the moment was shattered by the outside world.

Fergus closed his eyes for a second and then his lips curved ruefully. 'I'm not on call. Stay here. I'll be back.'

He slid from beneath the sheet and then covered Ailee's shoulder as he sat on the edge of the bed. He picked up the phone and with his other hand he tucked the sheet around her neck.

Ailee watched him, watched his face, listened to his voice and decoded the expressions on his face. He'd have to go and they would postpone this again, but her time would come and everything would be fine. Her doubts had gone.

Fergus replaced the receiver. 'There's a problem. I do have to go.'

'I know.'

He leant across and kissed her forehead. 'Do you want to stay here?'

'No. I'll go home.'

'I'll ring you. There is no doubt we have to talk.' Fergus glanced around at the clothes scattered across the floor and his eyes twinkled. 'We do seem to have trouble keeping our clothes on around each other.'

She blushed but held her head high to meet his teasing. 'It's a lovely failing.'

Ailee slid out of the bed and wrapped the sheet

around her body as he moved into the dressing room. She stood up, gathered her clothes and began to dress.

William was late home and when he came in he brushed Ailee's concern off and went straight to bed, complaining of cramps. Fergus rang to ask her out for dinner but Ailee couldn't help the feeling that something was wrong with William and she needed to get to the bottom of it. She couldn't leave William while he was unwell.

Fergus frowned at the phone. 'Your brother is sick?' Ailee sounded quite distracted, which wasn't like her. 'Is there anything I can do?'

'Not yet, but maybe later.' There was dryness in her tone he didn't appreciate but she didn't need him to push her.

'I'll ring tomorrow, then.'

'Thank you for understanding, Fergus.' He didn't understand anything, except she couldn't talk to him because her brother was sick.

By Sunday William was still unwell, which was unusual after dialysis. Ailee nagged her reluctant brother into a return to the hospital for a check-up.

Her years of renal medicine blurred when William was involved but she suspected her brother's condition could cause more delays for their surgery. He needed to be well by Wednesday's assessment clinic or who knew what Fergus would decide?

That evening saw William admitted to hospital as an emergency and the duty doctor refused to meet Ailee's eyes. He asked her to leave while he carried out the examination.

When the doctor had finished, William looked even more subdued, and Ailee had been fobbed off to see Mr McVicker in the morning.

Ailee's feeling that not all was right with William strengthened.

First thing on Monday morning Ailee heard Jody had been readmitted through Casualty with signs of rejection of her new kidney and pancreas, which meant Ailee had no chance to talk to Fergus.

The ward was on tenterhooks as they waited for their star patient to arrive, and Ailee went about her duties with a dark heart. First William unwell and now Jody.

Ailee met Fergus's eyes as Jody was wheeled into the ward and they both knew she was headed for High Dependency.

Jody lay in the emergency bed and she looked terrible. Her face was flushed and the rigors of her body were shaking the rails on the bed in time to the chattering of her teeth.

'Get some bloods and get another line in,' Fergus said as he reached for the phone. 'Who sent her to the ward? She needs to get to ICU immediately.'

Jody opened her eyes and squinted up a Fergus. 'Don't let me reject my kidney, Mr McVicker. I so want to be well. I don't want to let my donor down.'

'You haven't let anyone down, Jody. We'll do everything we can. Try and rest, sweetheart. Close your eyes and leave it to us.'

The ward round was postponed and, like the emergency with Emma, Ailee itched to be back on the medical team and follow Fergus and Jody up to Intensive Care. The next few hours would be critical. They could lose at least her kidney, if not the pancreas, and if infection set in they could even lose Jody.

In her office, Ailee tried to concentrate on the paper-work essential to the donor-recipient records and even managed to complete the full list of recipients for Marion and John's daughter, Eva, which she would need later in the day.

Ailee was scheduled to meet Eva's parents after lunch. Already she had three thank-you letters to give to them from the families of people whose lives had been enormously changed by Eva's gift.

All through the morning Ailee buried herself in the tasks she needed to complete and when she finally made her way to Intensive Care Jody was on life support and her family was there. Fergus had just left to do a delayed ward round and that meant Ailee couldn't stay. She hugged Jody's mother and hurried back to the ward.

By the time she arrived, Fergus had started the round without her. She came in as Fergus and Lawrence were discussing his discharge.

'If you feel your spirits dropping, you need to contact your support worker,' Fergus said.

Lawrence looked up and smiled at Ailee. 'Hi, Ailee. Have you told Mr McVicker what you've got me doing now?'

Fergus glanced across and gave Ailee a half-smile as if he wasn't willing to broadcast to the world how glad he was to see her.

'I haven't had a chance this morning.' She looked at Fergus. 'Lawrence has enrolled in a correspondence welfare course and is offering to mentor some of the young patients we have with compliance problems as soon as he finishes his course. If they listen to anyone, it will be someone who understands like Lawrence does.'

'Sounds promising. Keep me posted. Well done, both of you.' The entourage moved on and William was next.

'Not been well, William?'

William shook his head and closed lacklustre eyes.

'Let's have a look at you, then.' Rita stepped in and pulled the curtains around Fergus, William and herself.

Ailee sighed and stared at the screens around William and she could hear Fergus murmuring. When the curtains opened she looked up to see the verdict.

'If we can get him a little better, I think we'll be fine for next week. But a lot of that will be up to you, William.'

Ailee sighed with relief and then Fergus went on, 'Contact his donor.' He scanned down the page for the donor's name, and then his expression froze.

'Any relation?' The question ignored everyone else in the room and it seemed time slowed to a frame at a time as Fergus's eyes bored into hers. Ailee felt as though she was on the witness stand but she'd done nothing wrong.

CHAPTER NINE

AILEE licked dry lips. 'I am the donor.'

'And William?' Fergus's eyes burned into hers.

Ailee looked at William sitting up in bed, pale and listless and watching both of them. 'Is my only brother.'

'I see.' Fergus looked away from her to William and tried to smile. He felt as though all the air had been sucked out of the room and a tight band across his chest wouldn't allow him to breathe in again.

He looked at the boy. William had Ailee's colouring but had missed out on her height. He had a similar smile to his sister, though, and it made it even harder for Fergus to grapple with what he'd just learned. It explained a lot but now wasn't the time to sort it out.

The whole team watched and to strangle Ailee would not be a good look at this moment.

The rest of the group did not give the impression this was startling news so he gathered he'd been the only one in the dark.

Fergus turned to Rita, who was trying valiantly to appear uninterested in the byplay between Ailee and himself. 'Make sure Dr Green has the final blood tests and cross-match attended.' He turned back to William and met his eyes. 'I'll be keeping an eye on your results, too, young man. You'd better stay in hospital tonight as well.'

William was not happy at having to stay in hospital, but could see Fergus would not be interested in negotiation at that moment.

Ailee bit her lip. She'd thought she'd feel better once Fergus knew but she could only regret not having told him earlier. He had been genuinely shocked. She'd have to worry about that later because he was moving on to the next room and she needed to keep up.

Peter and Emma were both doing well and served to redirect the focus.

'How are you, Emma?' Fergus forced himself to smile at the young woman who already had more colour in her cheeks.

'I'm feeling much better. This would have been my dialysis day and I didn't have to go.'

'New kidneys are clever organs.' This time the smile came easier and Fergus glanced through her chart. Good scenarios did happen. 'Everything is perfect. Just get your strength back. You should be able to go home next week if all goes well.'

'What about you, Peter?' The young man looked pale. Fergus concentrated on the donor more than he ever had. From the donor's point of view, they'd done the job and were old news now.

Fergus realised he'd always been concerned that the donor recovered well but his obsession had been the recipient. With the news of Ailee's plan to be a donor that thought process had already suffered a subtle change.

'I'm fine, Mr McVicker. When can I go home?'

Fergus narrowed his eyes. The young man seemed to be quite exhausted and was in obvious discomfort. 'Home at the end of this week if all goes well. Is there a rush?'

Peter smiled weakly. 'Not really. It's just my dad is finding it hard to run the shop and if I even went in and sat in there, I could help a little.'

'You really can't do a lot for a few weeks at the very least, Peter. You have had a major operation and at a guess you're not taking enough pain medication.' Fergus glanced at Rita, who confirmed his suspicion.

'It makes me sleepy.'

'That's right. Take it. Sleep. Recover. That's an order.'

Peter looked sheepishly at Fergus and smiled slightly. 'If you say so.'

Fergus looked at Rita. 'I want him given analgesics on a regular basis. The weight of the world will wait till he's a little better.' He looked at Rita. 'And push those beds together so they can hold hands.' Everybody smiled at Fergus's teasing.

Fergus didn't feel like laughing at all, and as soon as the round was over he intended to have a little chat with Dr Ailee Green.

A few minutes later the group broke up and Fergus took Ailee's arm and steered her into the office. He shut the door to the ward before she knew what was happening. The air in the room seemed to shimmer with his icy calm.

Fergus's eyes chilled her. 'Let's go back to when we

spent time together in Singapore.' He waited for a moment, as if she needed time to recall, and then he went on.

'Why didn't you tell me you were booked as a live donor and that was the reason you didn't want to see me in Sydney?'

Ailee flicked a quick glance at the closed door, as if judging the distance, but she knew he deserved to know. She could feel the thudding in her chest but she refused to admit he had her off balance.

She lifted her eyes to his. 'In Singapore, you didn't tell me you were a leading renal specialist.'

Fergus was nowhere near satisfied with that answer. 'Lame. You didn't ask!'

She tilted her chin. 'Lame yourself. You avoided the information. As I did! In Singapore my impending operation wasn't something I discussed with passing strangers.'

Fergus shook his head. 'We were more than strangers!'

Ailee raised her chin higher. 'Passing holiday romance, you mean?'

He looked away and she knew that what she'd said was true. 'I had to be here to support my mother and William, be the strong one and not divert their attention from any effects on me for the next few months. I chose to deal with one issue at a time and if that put paid to a liaison with a man I met on the plane, then so be it.'

'I'm beginning to think you deliberately misled me.'

He went on without completing that train of thought. 'So this is why you're doing a temporary job. Because you'll be off work for the next couple of months, recovering?'

'That's right. It's the least I can do for the unit.'

He nodded but not at anything she'd said. It was as if he'd just confirmed something to himself.

'And the last week you couldn't tell me?'

'I've tried for the last three days.'

'Earlier would have been better. Yesterday was the first effort I've seen, but it's out now.'

He laughed without humour. 'Define irony. A kidney surgeon falls for a live donor and she's reluctant to risk a relationship because she's donating a kidney.'

'You and your daughter don't need another tragedy in your lives.'

His face twisted into a cynical smile. 'Sophie is definitely a concern. This bears more discussion, Ailee. Let's say I'll pick you up at five. And by the way, I want a psychological and psychiatric assessment done on William a.s.a.p.'

Ailee's head was still spinning from the impending discussion at five. She frowned. This could slow everything down again. 'He's already had one, a few months ago.'

'And he can have another. I have concerns he may not be mentally ready for this.'

Ailee couldn't believe what she was hearing. 'You can't postpone our operations!'

'I'll pretend you didn't say that, Doctor,' Fergus said very quietly, and then walked out of the room.

Ailee sagged back against the wall.

So much for everything being fine. Fergus had found out in the worst possible way and now he was angry with her. She just hoped he wouldn't take it out on William. She shook her head. Of course he wouldn't.

Fergus walked out of the ward, around the side of the hospital and down to the shady area reserved for smokers. Thankfully, the area was deserted, and he could have a few moments to himself.

Lord knew, he needed time to come to grips with this.

Live donor. People did it all the time. He advocated it. He had travelled halfway across the world in a flimsy plane to discover new ways to promote live donations in Australia. Now he had one on his own doorstep that he didn't want.

'Ironic' wasn't a big enough word. Would it have been better if he'd known this yesterday before he'd taken Ailee home to his bed? Would he have distanced himself from her because of this?

He doubted it. It was a shock and he could even begin to see her side of the dilemma, but he'd been hooked on Ailee since Singapore and it didn't change the way he felt about her.

But this sure as hell complicated things. Concern about Ailee's operation was the last thing his daughter needed now she'd started to trust him again.

Ailee walked out of the office and straight into Rita.

Rita took one look at her and glanced around to see if anyone else had noticed Ailee's pallor. 'You OK, kiddo?'

'I'm fine.'

'So he wasn't thrilled to find you were the donor.'

'I think he's just disappointed I didn't tell him before-hand, seeing as I work here and everyone else knew.'

'Is that what it was?' Rita didn't sound convinced but she didn't labour the point. 'What time is your appointment with the Ellises?'

Ailee looked at her watch. 'Another half-hour, but I need to check one last recipient.' Ailee chewed her lip. 'We need to arrange another psychological and psychiatric assessment of William on Mr McVicker's orders.'

'I'll do that.' Rita didn't seem to have a problem or think it unusual that Fergus had requested a repeat assessment. Maybe she was being paranoid.

She heard herself say 'Mr McVicker' when she thought of him as Fergus and that sounded strange, too. It wasn't the only thing weird about her relationship with Fergus but one of many. She didn't have time or the headspace to worry about it. She'd find out where she stood soon enough. Five o'clock, to be exact.

'If you hear any more about Jody, let me know, will you?' Ailee glanced at her watch again. It was time she headed back to her office. Her problems were nothing compared to those of the couple she was about to see.

The Ellises looked worn down by grief and Ailee hugged them both. 'Thank you so much for coming.'

Marion sighed as she sat in one of the two chairs in front of Ailee's desk. 'I know you said you'd come to us, Ailee, but we needed to get out. This visit gave us some purpose today.'

Mr Ellis nodded as he sat beside his wife. 'We're finding it hard to start the day at the moment. Everyone tells us that in time we'll remember more good times, but we're not there yet.'

Ailee felt helpless in the face of their grief. There was so little she could do to ease their pain. 'Nobody expects you to be able to function normally.'

She shuffled the papers in her hand. 'Would you like to know about the recipients? I do have three letters here from the families of recipients whose lives have been changed. Please, don't read them until you feel you are able to.'

Marion looked at her husband and then back at Ailee and nodded. 'Tell us a little if you can, please, Ailee.'

'I can tell you that Eva has saved the life of a fifteen-year-old-girl with cystic fibrosis. This young woman would have died within the next week or two if not for Eva. Her parents are beside themselves with joy that she will now get better.'

Marion smiled with great effort. 'That is wonderful news. Isn't it, John?'

John nodded, unable to speak, and reached into his pocket for his handkerchief.

Marion sniffed and lifted her chin a little higher. 'Is there more you can tell us?'

'One of Eva's kidneys and her pancreas went to a twenty-two-year-old woman in Melbourne who is studying to be a doctor and had been sick for two years. She was also a diabetic, like the girl I told you about last week, so had the double transplant. She is doing so well she may go home at the end of next week.'

They were all silent for a moment as they tried to envisage what it meant to the recipient.

Ailee went on because she decided it would be better to get it all over as soon as possible. 'The other kidney went to a twenty-five-year-old man whose wife had died. He has two little boys, so the difference to that family is incredible.'

Marion looked at her husband. 'Imagine if we hadn't agreed and all that good was wasted.'

'It is always a hard decision,' Ailee said.

'Can you tell us more?' John had recovered his composure and was trying hard to support his wife.

'There is one more. The other person is a thirty-year-old woman, struck down with keratoconus, which is an eye disease where the central cornea bulges forward and prevents light from being focussed correctly into the eye.'

Ailee sketched a quick diagram of an eye to explain the problem. 'The only substitute for replacing a human cornea is a human cornea.' She looked up to see that they understood.

'This lady has been blind for eighteen months, lost her job and struggled to look after herself, and now, thanks to Eva, has had her sight restored and can lead a normal life.'

Ailee handed across an envelope. 'All the information I can give you is on that sheet but I think it would be too much to take in now. Just know that you did the right thing and Eva has irrevocably touched these people's lives and she will never be forgotten.'

'And we can't contact them, can we?'

Ailee shook her head. 'No. I'm sorry. But I can send on any letters they or you want to send and there is an independent register you can leave your name with.

Later, if any of the recipients want to contact you, they can register with them as well.'

John nodded and looked at Marion. 'We'll think about it. A few months down the track perhaps.'

Ailee smiled gently. 'Don't rush anything. You can ring me any time. If I'm not available, someone else will get back to you as soon as we can. I understand Eva's funeral is tomorrow?'

John cleared his throat. 'We wanted to tell people about the families Eva's request has helped. Maybe then even more people will agree to sign donor cards in the future.'

Marion added. 'That way Eva's legacy will continue to grow.' Marion leant forward to lever herself up from her chair and her husband jumped up to help her.

Ailee stood as well. 'That is a wonderful idea. I will be thinking of you both tomorrow.'

'Thank you for your help, Ailee.'

Ailee hugged them both. 'Thank you from me, Mr McVicker, all the staff here and especially the people whose lives Eva has changed.'

Ailee watched them go and sighed. She remembered when her father had died suddenly and her family had gone through the shocking grief that surrounded the loss of a loved one.

The gathering of family, friends and even strangers had helped more than she'd believed possible. She hoped it would be that way for the Ellises tomorrow.

Her phone rang and it was a transplant co-ordinator from a southern Sydney hospital with a kidney available for one of her patients on the waiting list. Another tragedy like the Ellises'. Ailee couldn't help wincing, but it was another ray of hope for those in need.

Ailee looked up her records and dialled the number of the proposed recipient.

Thirty-eight-year-old Stephen Ward had been on dialysis for three years while he'd waited for a kidney and he couldn't believe it when Ailee phoned him with the news.

'So I have to come in now?' Stephen's voice betrayed his disbelief and growing excitement.

'Yes, please, Stephen. As soon as you can without getting a speeding ticket. You're only about half an hour away. Don't eat or drink anything and we'll start work-up as soon as you get here.'

'I'm on my way. Wait till I tell my wife.'

Ailee smiled at the waves of exhilaration coming through the phone. 'Just remember, sometimes things change. Don't get over-excited until we can guarantee you're going in.'

'I'll try not to—but it's hard. See you soon.'

Ailee put the phone down and looked up Fergus's page number, then decided she'd ring Rita to prepare the ward first. Coward.

Rita was quick to answer and too soon there was Fergus to be notified, and then the theatre when the surgeon had a time he was available. Fergus would ring the anaesthetists.

When her phone rang she knew it was Fergus answering his page, and she couldn't speak for a second as she gathered her thoughts.

'Did you page me, Ailee?'

Ailee licked dry lips. 'Yes. We have a donor kidney and match available for today. What time would you like Theatre organised for?'

'Make it two this afternoon. That should give the recipient time to fast and have the work-up. I'll have my secretary reschedule the afternoon appointments in my rooms for later.'

Ailee bit her lip and wondered if she, too, would get a reprieve.

Fergus must have read her mind. His voice dropped. 'Don't even think about it. It means our appointment will be rescheduled. I'll pick you up from your place at eight. If I'm late, I'll still be coming.'

Ailee swallowed. 'We could put that off until tomorrow.'

'No,' he said succinctly. 'Anything else?'

Ailee pulled a face at the phone but her voice remained composed. 'That's all, thank you.'

'I'll see you later, then.'

His receiver clicked and Ailee put her own phone down. Today was going to be another big day.

Ailee gathered the enormous amounts of paperwork needed for Stephen Ward's transplant operation and headed for the ward.

She couldn't help going over the conversation she'd just had with Fergus as she walked, and she reasoned that if he'd considered her planned operation an insurmountable problem he wouldn't be in that much of a hurry to clear the air. Maybe everything wasn't as bad as she thought it was.

* * *

Fergus arrived at Ailee's house at exactly eight p.m. Ailee knew because she'd been watching the clock for the last hour and she'd only just checked the time again.

'I'm going out now, Mum,' she called through to the sitting room where Helen was watching television.

The doorbell rang before she could get to it and she muttered under her breath. She'd hoped to keep Fergus and her mother apart.

Ailee opened the door before Fergus had finished ringing. 'I'm ready. Let's go.'

'What's your rush?' He looked tall and gorgeous and totally in command and refused to move away from the door. 'I'd like to meet your mother.'

Ailee glared at him, but she was really annoyed at herself for being so glad to see him there when she should be keeping him away from her mother.

'Who's there, dear?' Helen's voice floated through to the front door.

Fergus just stared back with slightly raised eyebrows. 'Don't you think there have been enough secrets, Ailee?' he said.

Ailee sighed and turned to call over her shoulder. 'It's Fergus McVicker.' She resisted the urge to grit her teeth at Fergus. 'Would you like to meet him?'

Helen appeared and Ailee moved back to allow Fergus to step into the tiled entry.

Fergus smiled warmly and held out his hand. 'Hello, Mrs Green. I'm Fergus. I work with Ailee.' He shook hands and Ailee's mother blushed prettily.

'Call me Helen. It's lovely to finally meet you, Fergus. You've featured in a lot of our conversations this week.'

Fergus lifted his eyebrows and looked at Ailee. 'Really?'

'William is a constant concern at the moment, as you know.' Ailee refused to bite. She glanced at her watch. 'I won't be long, Mum.'

'Take your time, dear. I'm off to bed now anyway. Nice to meet you, Fergus.'

'Good to meet you, too, Helen'

Ailee watched her mother colour again and she sympathised. Fergus being charming was hard not to like but Ailee was learning.

Finally seated in the car, the silence was strained as they pulled out from the kerb. Ailee drew a breath to make her feelings known but he sidetracked her with his own schedule.

Fergus glanced across. 'I have to call in at the hospital. I think Jody will be fine, but I want to check her one more time tonight.'

The young recipient had been at the back of Ailee's mind all evening. 'Can I come up to the ward with you? Just to have a peek. I won't go in and see her.'

He glanced across again. 'I don't have a problem with that—it's up to you.'

When they arrived at the hospital Ailee followed Fergus up to Intensive Care, where he gowned and gloved before entering the isolation room. Jody was being treated with huge doses of steroids and the strongest immunosuppressants to prevent her body rejecting the donor kidney, but it left Jody's system easy prey to bacteria and viruses.

Ailee spoke to the registered nurse at the desk and

watched Fergus through the glass as he spoke to Jody and the nurse specialling her.

'So she's improving?'

'When he was here earlier, Mr McVicker seemed to think this acute rejection phase was settling. Her observations are stable and her counts are down.'

Ailee could see that Fergus was preparing to leave. 'Fingers crossed. I'll pop up and see her parents tomorrow.'

The nurse nodded. 'So what are you doing here? Are you with Mr McVicker for fun, or are there more transplants on the cards?' They both looked across at the other glassed-in room.

Ailee forced a smile. Frivolity was far from the case. 'Not for fun, but no transplants tonight so far. How is our latest patient? Stephen OK?'

'Looking good. His wife is a sweetie. They're a lovely couple to see such a good result for.'

Ailee nodded, aware that Fergus was waiting for her. 'Better go. Thanks for your help.'

Ailee crossed the room with relief. She hoped the nurse assumed they were there together on renal business because she wasn't ready to be the subject of a gossip storm. It had become a little tricky at the end.

'Shall I take your arm?' Fergus teased, well aware Ailee was trying to give the impression everything was businesslike between them.

'No. Thank you. I have to work here and you'll be going back to your own hospital in a week or two.'

'That will be a good thing,' Fergus said quietly.

Ailee looked across at him and wondered what that statement meant.

They didn't speak again until Fergus pulled up outside a trendy restaurant overlooking the moonlit beach.

'I thought a late supper would be in order as I haven't eaten. You could have dessert if you're not hungry.'

Ailee bit her lip. So he'd been working non-stop. 'That would be lovely. Of course you have to eat. Now I feel guilty I didn't offer you something when you came to pick me up.'

'Guilt is good.' Fergus smiled and held the door of the restaurant open for her. So he wasn't angry with her any more. It was nice to banter and she could get used to waiters rushing to assist her.

They were seated quickly at a reserved table and Ailee glanced around at the few couples still seated.

'This is very stylish,' Ailee said. 'I was thinking you'd want somewhere more private to vent your feelings.'

'I'm a very stylish guy,' he teased, 'and if I took you back to my home, I wasn't sure we'd get any talking done.'

Ailee willed the heat not to rise in her face but her cheeks burned. 'It takes two.'

'Absolutely,' Fergus said, straight-faced, and caught the waiter's eye to order.

Ailee chose a sorbet and Fergus a rare steak and salad and the food arrived in minutes. They discussed Jody's stabilisation and Stephen's operation, and Ailee couldn't help remembering how good it was to have Fergus to bounce ideas off.

As soon as he'd finished eating, Fergus returned to the issues they had been skirting all night.

'So what are we going to do about this deadly attraction between us?'

Ailee looked down at the remains of her sorbet. 'Is the attraction deadly?'

Fergus waited until she was forced to look at him to break the silence and then he said, 'I admit to some homicidal thoughts when I discovered the tiny fact you hadn't mentioned.'

Ailee lifted her chin. 'You said any secret I had wouldn't change the way you felt.'

'And I meant it.' He allowed his words to settle between them and sink in.

He changed tack. 'Why was it so hard for you to tell me about William?'

Ailee stared ahead out the window to the moonlight sparkling off the waves. 'There are many reasons. Some major and some minor reasons, important to me and not to others.'

'Such as?' She had his full attention.

She shrugged. 'The next few weeks of discomfort I'll be less than wonderful company. Physically I'll have restrictions for the first few months and I guess I'll have changes in body image to come to terms with, although that's a minor consideration. I certainly haven't had second thoughts.'

'Not too minor when it's your own body, but go on.'

She glanced back at him, unsure what he meant, but his face didn't help her understand.

She went on, 'William should be watched closely and I'll need to stay on standby until he's right. I don't want what happened to Emma to happen to William. That commitment to my family is no way to start a relationship with someone.'

'I'm sure we could manage to cope. Then again, not everyone has a sister who specialises in renal surgery and those recipients seem to survive. You haven't convinced me.'

She faced him. 'All right, then. Mostly I don't think it's fair to you and Sophie. There are risks, not huge risks statistically but risks nevertheless.'

She was glad to get this off her chest. 'You've already told me how long it's taken Sophie to resume normal life after losing her mother. If she were to see me debilitated, it is likely I could bring all those painful memories back for her.'

Fergus took a few moments to reply and then he spoke slowly, as if being careful of what he said. 'I can see that is a possibility and it is something I need to address. It was one of the first things I thought about when I finally found out about your relationship with William. Sophie is to be protected at all costs.'

Ailee agreed. She'd always thought that but it stung nonetheless that she would always be second or perhaps even third in his life after his dead wife.

These were all reasons she should have stayed away from him in Singapore. Funny how the closer she became to Fergus the more obstacles she could see. And the more of him she needed and selfishly wanted.

'Why didn't you want me to meet your mother this evening?' His question jolted her out of her meanderings and she spoke without thought.

'Sophie isn't the only one who needs protecting.'

'*Touché.*'

Fergus acknowledged the hit and Ailee sighed and went on. 'Why broadcast my somewhat tenuous relationship with you before William's operation? If Mum thought I was entering a relationship, she would revisit the possible ramifications on my life, fertility and health again.'

Fergus tilted his head. 'Your mother is entitled to her valid concerns.'

Ailee frowned. 'You are the last person I would expect to be unenthusiastic about donating to help another person. Do you have concerns?'

'Honestly?' He looked across at her and his eyes softened. 'If I didn't know you so well, the statistics tell me there is nothing to worry about, or about one in thirty thousand as in any operation. Knowing you doesn't change that, but somehow it does.'

He glanced out the window and then back at Ailee. 'I'd be lying if I said I wasn't worried. I've already lost someone dear to me from such a low risk.'

He went on, 'But I can see you are determined and I'll be glad, as you will be, when it's all over.'

He sighed and deliberated on voicing what was on his mind. 'If the operation goes ahead, that is.'

Ailee looked unutterably relieved to finally have her concerns out in the open so there was a delay until she'd comprehended his last sentence. He watched her expression change to one of disbelief and regretted the necessity of burdening her.

'What do you mean, if the operation goes ahead? We're booked in next week.'

Fergus spread his fingers on the table. 'You haven't seen the paperwork. William's psychological assessment wasn't good. I don't know how you missed it but William is exhibiting all the signs of denial and non-compliance.'

Ailee shook her head vehemently. 'No, he's not!'

Fergus went on softly but remorselessly. 'You know that the first criterion a kidney recipient needs to meet is compliance. We have to be sure he is not going to throw this chance away by breaking the very stringent rules and medication regime post-operatively. We would do him no favours if we allow him to waste this chance.'

'I can't believe what I'm hearing.' She shook her head in further denial. 'How dare you say William is non-compliant? He's never missed a clinic or dialysis and lord knows, it's painful enough for him.'

Fergus knew he was losing her and the familiar pain swept over him. There had been so many ups and down with this relationship but he was responsible for the optimum outcome for his patients, and like hell he'd waste Ailee's kidney if her brother wasn't going to value it as he should.

'I'm sorry, Ailee. It is true. William has been binge-drinking alcohol and eating what he likes. His fluid quota has been consistently over and his biochemistry is totally out of whack.'

'No. He couldn't. He wouldn't.' She searched her memory and a few minor incidents gnawed at her confidence.

Fergus went on. 'Don't tell me that—look at his pathology results. You need to ask why he would jeopardise his transplant.'

Ailee shook her head again but fear was like a hard rock in her chest. 'I do not, for a moment, believe this is true. But, if it were, what possible reason could he have to do that?'

Fergus reached across to take her hand but she pulled her fingers out of his reach, unable to tolerate his sympathy, and the gulf between them widened.

Ailee went on without allowing Fergus to speak. 'He has no reason to do that.'

'He might.' Fergus pulled his coffee-cup closer and added sugar very slowly as if to give her time to calm down.

'What about guilt?' he suggested. 'Concern for you and fears he can't cope with? Dread of rejection and that your sacrifice would all be for nothing? There are a hundred issues more mature people than William can't face. If he is too unwell for transplant, he doesn't have to admit any of those fears.'

Ailee planted her hands on the table. 'It's not true. I think you're just making this up so I won't have the operation.'

His face didn't change. 'That is not true, Ailee. What possible reason could I have for that?'

She sniffed. 'You tell me. Is your professional judgement clouded by other issues?'

Fergus sat back as if she'd slapped him. 'You don't believe that.'

Ailee covered her mouth with her hands and drew a deep breath before she spoke. This was all her fault for becoming involved with Fergus and not concentrating on William.

'I don't know what to believe. I need to think. I need to talk to William and I need space from you. I knew a relationship with you wouldn't work. I want to go home.'

'As you wish.' He signalled for the cheque. 'William's problems need discussion and I regret I've upset you. I know this a shock and maybe you do need some time alone to come to terms with your disappointment.'

The drive home was accomplished in silence and Ailee opened her own door before Fergus could get out. She didn't think he was surprised.

'Thank you.'

'For what?'

'For agreeing to give me space.' She shut the car door, walked up the front path and didn't look back.

There wasn't a lot she could do this late at night and she wasn't going to think about Fergus. The hospital wouldn't thank her for waking up William and she couldn't share this with her mother.

Had William been drinking and consciously or sub-consciously jeopardising his transplant chances? How had she missed that he was having second thoughts?

Or was she justified in her accusation that Fergus was seeing things that were not there because he'd already lost one woman in surgery and he was frightened to lose another?

She needed to talk to her brother and sort this out.

She knew she'd been unfair to Fergus but this was all part of the reason she hadn't wanted to get involved in the first place.

He steamrollered her, clouded the issue and confused her, and took her strength when she needed it most. She should have stayed away from him. This was all her fault for not concentrating on William. She'd been side-tracked by her own dilemmas but she'd change. She wouldn't make the same mistake again.

When Fergus arrived home it was ten o'clock and he knew he wouldn't sleep.

Ailee had been devastated and he guessed she would blame herself for not noticing William's deviation earlier and probably he himself for telling her.

Just so long as she didn't blame him if the decision to transplant was rescinded. He hoped Dr Harry would be back for that one.

Light was still angling from beneath Sophie's door and he knocked gently in case she had fallen asleep, reading.

'Hello, Dad.' His daughter sat up in bed.

'Hello, sweetheart. What are you doing awake?'

She glanced at the clock as if to say he was the late one. 'I wanted to wait for you to come home.'

'I'm home. Now go to sleep. It's school tomorrow.' Fergus crossed the room and pulled the curtains before coming back to sit on the edge of the bed.

'I know. Did you have a nice night with Ailee?' Sophie was smirking at him as if she'd caught him out.

He appreciated her cleverness but discussing Ailee with his daughter was the last thing on his wish list. 'What makes you think I was with Ailee?'

'Intuition.'

He raised his eyebrows and suppressed a smile. 'Really? What else does your intuition tell you?'

Sophie tilted her head on one side and studied him.

The mannerism belonged to her mother and Fergus accepted the twinge of regret that would always be there for the loss of the first woman he'd ever loved.

'Things are not going smoothly,' his daughter pronounced.

'You have wonderful intuition, just like your mother had.' He tucked in her bedclothes. 'I love you but I'm not going to discuss this with you. Now, go to sleep.'

'Dad?'

This time he did smile. 'Yes, Sophie.'

'Occasionally you have to take risks if something is important enough.'

'Thank you, baby. I'll remember that.' He leant across and kissed his daughter on the brow. 'Goodnight.'

''Night, Dad.'

In the morning Sophie was up before he left, which was unusual, and she dragged her fluffy slippers across the floor as she entered.

She shuffled across the room and slumped into the chair next to him. 'I had a bad dream last night.'

Fergus put down his coffee and concentrated on his daughter. She looked pale.

'You OK?' Fergus said. Sophie shook her head and now that he looked properly he saw that her eyes were red.

'Not really,' she said softly.

Fergus stood up, pulled his daughter up against him and put his arms around her. She didn't pull away and felt soft and forlorn in his arms. He dreaded the times in the future when their rapport might be lost again.

For the moment she trusted him again and he

accepted how much he needed that trust from his daughter. 'Do you want to tell me about it?'

She nodded her head and he smoothed the hair back from her forehead. 'OK. Take your time.'

Sophie leant against him and then finally she mumbled into his shirt, 'Is Ailee sick?'

Fergus felt like groaning. 'Why do you ask?'

'Because in the dream she was sick like Mummy was. I was locked out of the room, looking through a window. You were sad and I was calling out to you, but you couldn't hear me.' Sophie buried her nose in his chest.

Fergus winced and rubbed her back. 'I will always hear you, baby.'

Sophie looked up at him with tear-filled eyes. 'So Ailee isn't sick—is she?'

Now he was in a dilemma. 'No. Ailee isn't sick.' He felt his daughter relax against him with relief and he hugged her briefly. He wasn't lying but he wasn't being fair to his daughter either. 'Ailee's brother is sick.'

Sophie stiffened against him. 'Can she catch it?'

He sighed. 'William is eighteen, and has end-stage renal failure. You are probably one of the few girls in your school who would understand what that is and what it means to a previously healthy young person.' He paused.

Sophie nodded and he drew a breath.

'Ailee is donating one of her kidneys to him in a week or two.'

Sophie froze and then pulled away to stare up into his face. 'But she might need it some time herself.'

He tried to smile. 'Ailee is very healthy.'

Sophie shook her head violently from side to side. 'Tell her she can't do it.'

He sighed and looked down at his daughter. She was so young and fragile and had been through so much. 'I can't tell her that. It's Ailee's decision.'

Sophie was still shaking her head. 'She could get sick. An infection or even a clot like Mummy! People die from operations. It's a big operation.'

'Ailee is not going to die.'

'Mummy wasn't supposed to die.'

Fergus ached for the young girl who had watched her mother go into the hospital and never come out. 'I know, darling.' He hugged Sophie to him but she pulled away.

'Why did you bring her here and make me like her if she's going to die?'

'I didn't make you like Ailee and she's not going to die.'

Sophie backed away out of his arms. 'Even if she doesn't die this time, one day she might get sick. She'll need her other kidney and it will be gone. Then she'll get sicker and sicker and die as well.'

Fergus stood there and watched his daughter back away from him. He tried to reason with her. 'Some people are born with one kidney and never have a problem. Perfectly healthy people who haven't donated can get sick kidneys suddenly. That is the same for everyone, Sophie.'

Sophie shook her head. 'You shouldn't have brought her here. I hate her and I hate you.' Sophie spun on her heel and ran out of the room, and Fergus rubbed his face with his hand. Terrific.

Ailee would be saying 'I told you so' and he had a big problem.

CHAPTER TEN

ON TUESDAY morning Ailee arrived at the ward at the same time as the trolley bearing the breakfast trays.

Tossing in her bed, unable to sleep, Ailee had promised herself she would stay focussed on William and only William. He had to have the transplant.

When she entered the ward her brother was just pulling himself up in bed to eat and he looked very pale.

'Good morning, William.' Ailee approached the bed and shifted his bedside table closer, unsure how to start the conversation.

'Ailee. You're early.' William studied his sister's face and something he saw there brought a look of wariness to his eyes. Ailee felt her stomach drop as he looked away from her.

He buttered his toast intently. 'Have you come to steal my breakfast?' His attempt at lightening the mood fell flat and Ailee didn't help out.

'No. I've come to ask you some questions.'

'Like what?' There was a touch of bravado in the response and Ailee sighed.

'Why have you been drinking alcohol when you know it is the wrong thing to do for your condition? I thought you understood that.'

He glared at her. 'Who told you I was doing that?'

She leant on the breakfast tray and tried to read his face. 'It doesn't matter if what they say is true. Is it true, William?'

He shrugged. 'I've had a few beers with the boys. Sometimes more than a few. That's all.'

Ailee shook her head. Her worst fears had been confirmed. 'I heard you've been consistently over your fluid limit and your biochemistry hit the roof.'

'Well, it won't matter if I get one of your healthy-as-Hades kidneys, now, will it? Your kidney will fix everything.'

'They'll cancel the op if you prove yourself non-compliant.' She thought she'd shock him with that but he just shrugged.

'What—no life-long corticosteroids and waiting for your ultimate sacrifice to stop working?'

Ailee bit her lip against the shock. What sort of sister was she not to have noticed he was in this state?

'How long have you felt like this?' She felt like crying.

'Since you came back. Go home, Ailee. I don't want to talk about it.' This new William was a stranger and she didn't know how to get through to him.

Ailee put her hand on his arm but he shook it off. 'We have to talk about it. What am I going to tell Mum?'

'Just leave it. Leave me. I'm not in the mood to talk about this.' His voice rose and Ailee bit her lip.

Ailee stood there with the blood draining away from

her face. She felt sick and faint and horrified at the way her brother was looking at her. She was doing no good here—making things worse even.

She turned away and almost bumped into the ward sister who had come across to see what William's raised voice was about.

'Everything OK?"

Ailee tried to smile. 'Fine. I'll be back later,' she said, and left the ward almost at a run.

Fergus watched from the other side of the office. He'd planned on speaking to William before he saw his sister, but it was too late now.

The good news was that Ailee didn't know that he had seen the incident. The bad news was that he couldn't go after her and offer comfort because she wouldn't thank him.

He needed to step back and give her the space she'd asked for. He had a glimmer of an idea that could perhaps help and didn't involve him, but that was all he could do.

Ailee went back to her office and sat in the chair with her head in her hands at the desk. Everything had been going so smoothly, or she'd thought it had. She'd been blind and stupid when she should have been watchful and focussed.

First Fergus and her loss of control in Singapore, which she still couldn't believe, then his secondment slap in the middle of her workplace. Her inability to say no to him had her head spinning and all the time she'd been diverted from seeing that William had gone into self-destruct mode.

She didn't know where to begin to make things right, except that she needed to stay away from Fergus.

Her mother would be devastated if they ran into problems at this late stage, but if she didn't tell her it would be more of a shock at the last minute.

And she started work in an hour.

How she was going to get through the day? This was the last place she felt like being. She'd just have to believe everything would turn out all right.

An hour later she was back on the ward. During the round Ailee noticed that Fergus avoided any discussion with her. He spoke most of the time with Rita and his registrar, often with the result that Rita had to ask Ailee to clarify some points, which Rita would then relay to Fergus.

Well, she'd asked him for space. It was a good thing, Ailee reminded herself as she stifled her own contrariness.

When they came to William, Ailee may as well not have been in the room. William refused to look at her and even Fergus noticed the strain between the siblings.

As they moved on, Ailee heard Fergus ask Rita to have the social worker see William today. Everything was going wrong. Finally the round was over and Ailee had to hurry to meet her first appointment.

Fergus watched her go. Maybe she was right. They would have been better to have left all this until later. He needed to make sure his daughter wasn't hurt as well.

Ailee's meeting was with a mother planning to donate one of her kidneys to her son.

All of Iris Wilson's blood work had been completed and her scans and X-rays had been normal.

'It seems a lot of tests just to be able to give a kidney to my own son, Ailee.' Iris looked at the already thick folder lying on Ailee's desk.

'I know, Iris. These are all necessary to make sure that you will be well after donating your kidney. We'd look pretty silly if you only had one kidney and we let you give it away.' Ailee held up the renal imaging studies and pointed.

'There are your two kidneys and this one shows the blood supply and structures in and around your kidneys, which are all normal.'

Iris looked vaguely at the dark pictures and shrugged. 'If you say so.' She frowned. 'Because my son and I match blood groups, it's a good sign, isn't it?'

Ailee agreed. 'To be the same type is the best, but even a blood type your antibodies won't fight with can be fine. People with O-type blood are still compatible to give but not receive from all the others, and AB-type blood, like yours and Greg's, can receive from A, B, or O.'

'So how do they tell if Greg's blood antibodies are going to fight with mine?'

'To cross-match, we take blood from you and Greg, separate it down, and the laboratory incubates your lymphocytes with Greg's serum. They look to see if Greg has antibodies ready to fight against your cells.' Ailee paused to allow Iris time to understand that concept.

'Antibodies that are already formed, called preformed antibodies, can cause acute rejection after transplant. If antibodies already exist, the transplant can't go ahead. That's why some people are on waiting lists for years and others seem to have managed to jump the queue.'

Iris nodded. 'I wondered about that.'

Ailee went on. 'It depends on the antibodies in the match as much if not more than how long you have been waiting.'

Iris squinted at the results Ailee had facing her. 'So Greg hasn't any preformed antibodies against my blood?'

Ailee smiled. 'None were found so that is the best news.'

'So when do they finally start talking about operation dates?' Iris sat back and folded her plump arms across her ample breasts.

'It takes quite a while for all the tests to come back, and because transplanted kidneys don't always last for a long time, we make as much use of the failing kidneys as we can. It is usual to wait until just before someone like Greg needs dialysis. Then we do the operation.'

'So he might need another transplant in the future. How long does a transplanted kidney last?'

'It can vary, and we hope each kidney lasts a very long time. The majority of donor kidneys last between fifteen and thirty or more years if they are not rejected. Live donor kidneys, like yours, seem to last longer than those from someone unrelated who has died.'

Iris nodded and Ailee went on. 'You must remember that the fifteen or thirty years we talk about means that someone like Greg can have a normal life in that time. Even a shorter time than that makes a huge difference to a chronically ill person's quality of life.'

'You mention rejection. That seems to be the big worry.'

'And infection. The renal experts believe it could depend on the amount of acute rejection episodes Greg might have as to how long his new kidney lasts and how well he will be. That's why we keep a watchful eye on him for a long time.'

Iris sighed. 'We seem to have been getting ready to do this for months and months. I just want it all to end.'

Ailee leant across and squeezed Iris's hand. 'I know. I've been waiting to do the same for my brother for more than a year. It is a nerve-racking time. I even travelled overseas for a few months because my brother didn't need the operation at the time, but he's ready now.' Ailee gritted her teeth as she said it. He'd better be.

Iris's eyes widened. 'So when do you go in?'

Ailee thought of her last conversation with Fergus about William and stamped down her reservations. 'We're waiting for the final go-ahead from the surgeon, but it should be next week.'

When Ailee went back to see William that afternoon, she was dreading another confrontation.

But a different brother waited for her. William smiled, somewhat sheepishly, but smiled nonetheless.

'I'm sorry, sis.'

Ailee felt the tears rush to her eyes and she stepped closer until William hugged her. She sighed against him and hugged him back fiercely. 'I'm so sorry I didn't see how you were feeling.'

William brushed his own damp eyes. 'I'm sorry I was such a jerk.'

Ailee smiled and sniffed. 'You aren't a jerk but you scared me.' She tilted her head. 'What changed your mind?'

William half laughed. 'Who.'

Ailee didn't understand 'OK. Who?'

'Lawrence.' William shrugged. 'He practically kicked my butt he was so amazed at my stupidity.'

'When did you meet Lawrence?'

'Mr McVicker introduced us.' William shook his head. 'And I thought I had it bad. Hell. Poor Lawrence, but don't tell him I said that.'

Ailee felt like hugging the absent patient. 'I won't, but what did he say?'

Lawrence had obviously made a big impression on William. 'It was what he knew. He knew what I was thinking and how I felt and it was pretty weird to hear it come from someone else's mouth. He said Mr McVicker wanted a commitment from me today or he would cancel the op.'

Ailee felt sick. 'So what did you do?'

William shook his head at the enormity of what could have happened.. 'I finally realised how much I wanted to get on with my life and how stupid I've been. I asked to see Mr McVicker and said I would look after your kidney more carefully than anyone else in the world. He said I'd better or he'd be gunning for me.'

He grinned. 'It looks like we're going to Theatre next week, sis.'

CHAPTER ELEVEN

ON WEDNESDAY, between ward rounds and transplant co-ordinator duties, Ailee was retested with another serum cross-match and tissue type to check that nothing had changed.

The new transplant co-ordinator would start on Monday and Ailee needed to ensure all her records and tasks were up to date. At least her workload meant she had little time to dwell on the disaster of her love life.

Any interaction with Fergus had dwindled to the barest minimum, and although he continued to treat everyone else with his usual warmth and care, Ailee was excluded from the circle with polite distance.

On the Friday before the surgery, both she and William underwent the final psychological testing to ensure they were mentally ready for the operation. This time the results came back resoundingly affirmative.

After a subdued weekend spent lazing around at home with her family, and no phone calls from Fergus,

Ailee was admitted on Monday afternoon as soon as William had his final dialysis.

This admission there was no fluid overload on William's part, even though both he and Ailee had been on a clear fluid diet for the last twenty-four hours.

Ailee unpacked her hospital bag in the single room allocated to her. She set up the bedside table for easy reach of things she imagined she might need when her movements would be severely restricted by the surgery.

As a quirk of her job, Ailee had quizzed Emma's husband, Peter, on any tips he might have for her for the post-operative period.

The morning of the operation finally arrived and Ailee woke up on the ward. Dr Harry was back and would perform Ailee's surgery. Fergus, on his last day at the hospital, would assist with William's transplant. Ailee was glad the surgical team had worked out as it had. Really glad.

Ailee could hear William's voice in the room next door as she slid her arms into her white hospital gown that threatened to expose everything to the world.

Her tummy rumbled more from nerves than the fact that she'd been fasting since midnight, and she imagined William felt the same.

'Morning, bro.' Ailee's nonchalance didn't quite come off but the new closeness with William excused that and they smiled at each other.

'Hungry?' William teased to hide his own nervousness, and they both looked up as the night sister came around with their charts to finalise the theatre requirements.

'I thought I'd find you in here, Ailee.' Greta had

settled them to bed the previous night and had bullied
Ailee into a sleeping tablet.

'I did sleep, Greta.' Ailee smiled at the nurse and she
grinned back.

'Good. That's much better than you harassing me all
night.' They both knew what she meant. 'A good sleep
helps down the track.'

Greta smiled at William and then Ailee. 'I need some
observations from both of you so pop back to bed
because Dr Harry will be in soon and I have to do my
duty before I go off.'

Ailee obediently went back to her room and climbed
up into the bed.

In her absence a basket of glorious Singapore orchids
had arrived. The fragile blooms perfectly matched her
fragile mood and the memories rushed back. Tears
clouded her vision.

Fergus watched Ailee's hand stretch out to touch the
velvet of a purple orchid and the tightness in his chest
prevented him from speaking. He cleared his throat and
moved from the wall.

'Hello, Ailee.' It was all he could manage at that
moment as the full impact of how close she was to going
to Theatre hit him in the heart—just like the day he'd
first seen her.

'The flowers are beautiful,' she said and he could
barely hear her voice for the rushing sound in his ears.
He wanted to sweep her up into his arms and carry her
away to safety, even though he knew the idea was
ridiculous.

He cleared his throat again. 'I hope you don't mind but I needed to wish you well before you go in.'

'Thank you.' Ailee turned away and tried to brush the tears away without him seeing, but he came up in front of her and rested his hands on her shoulders.

Unable to help himself, he bent and kissed her lips and tasted the salt. 'Staying away is the hardest thing, Ailee.'

Greta bustled into the room with her charts and Fergus stepped back as she spoke to the folders in her hand. 'So all we need is…' She looked up and blinked when she saw Fergus was in the room. 'Mr McVicker?'

'I'm just leaving.' He looked at Ailee. 'I'll be in William's theatre. Good luck.'

Their eyes met for a final lingering look and for a moment Ailee thought he was going to kiss her again, but then he left and Ailee watched him go.

She wondered what they would have said to each other if there had been more time. But they were out of time. She lifted her chin. 'So what do you need, Greta?'

Greta ticked the boxes on the pre-admission sheet. 'Just need to take your blood pressure and check your armband.'

Ailee nodded and lifted her arm.

An hour later Ailee lay on her back, slightly fuzzy from the pre-anaesthetic medication, on her way to the operating theatre. She'd always wondered what it would feel like to see the ceiling go past like she had seen it in the movies so many times.

The air-conditioning vents streamed by, faceless voices came and went from her peripheral vision, and it seemed to take for ever to arrive at the swinging plastic doors of the operating theatres.

A figure clad in a scrub suit took her hand and checked her armband. 'Hello. Can you tell me your name and what operation you are having today?' Ailee had heard it all so many times and now it was her turn.

After the check they passed through into the anaesthetic room and Andrew was all bouncy good humour.

'So, Ailee,' he said as he patted her wrist and squared up to impale her vein with an incredibly large cannula. 'bet you never thought you'd see me from this angle.'

'If you didn't have a mask on, I'd be able to see up your nose,' she bantered back, but the nerves were starting to squirm inside at what lay ahead and some of it must have shown in her eyes.

Andrew dropped his humour and patted her shoulder. 'You'll be fine, my friend. We need your sort around here. I'll take good care of you.'

'I know you will. Just make sure your colleague next door takes good care of William, too.'

'Done. Now, off you go to sleep.' And that was the last Ailee heard.

Fergus couldn't stay away as he waited for his own operation to start. He hovered around the theatre doors, not having been able to cope with the viewing-room window, and went over in his mind what would be happening inside.

Ailee lay in the theatre next door and William would come into this theatre when Ailee's kidney was ready. The scrub room lay between the two theatres.

Ailee's kidney would be removed first and the operation would take about an hour.

Fergus had checked and Dr Harry had chosen to use the open-excision method he'd used for thirty years. Fergus admitted to less chance of injury to the donor organ than the keyhole method of excision if the surgeon wasn't as used to laparoscopic nephrectomy.

He just wished Ailee hadn't had to suffer the extra recovery time, pain and movement restriction resulting from the large excision.

Although William's operation would take twice as long as Ailee's, Ailee would be the one with the extended recovery time and greater shock to the system because she'd previously been well.

William would start to feel better almost immediately.

But Fergus had no say—either in her choice of surgeon or anything to do with her life. She'd told him that.

An hour passed. 'What are you doing out here?' Dr Harry said as he slipped out of his sterile gown to have a small break before he had to re-scrub to assist Fergus with William's operation.

'Waiting for a friend. Is she out yet?'

The older surgeon smiled. 'I thought you might be. She's fine. And the young fellow will come along well, too.' He looked at Fergus from under his brows. 'She's just going through to Recovery now and isn't really awake. Go on through and see her.'

Fergus had been debating but Dr Harry was on a mission now. 'We can afford a few minutes before we start on young William. There has to be some bonus for all the extra hours we work.' Dr Harry's bushy eyebrows bounced up and down. 'So that's why you didn't want to do this one, eh?'

'As you say.' Fergus didn't enlarge on the subject and the older man didn't pursue it.

They entered the recovery area and Fergus picked out Ailee at twenty paces. She was asleep. Her face was pale and the IV was running a blood transfusion so she must have lost a bit. He sucked in his breath in shock.

Dr Harry heard the noise. 'She had a little bleeder, but we got it in the end.' He looked at Fergus and almost chuckled. 'She probably didn't need the blood but it saved her feeling tired for the next month so don't look at me like that.'

This was a common enough complication for patients, but not for Fergus, and not for Ailee. There was no escaping his need for this woman, and while he'd loved and mourned his first wife this was for now and the future, and his future revolved around Ailee.

There were obstacles before them but as he looked down at her, unconscious and moaning gently in her sleep, he vowed to himself he would have and hold his Ailee.

It might take time but Sophie would get used to the idea.

He moved across and lifted Ailee's hand to his cheek. She felt cold and he warmed her fingers between his hands before tucking them back under the covers.

He lifted his head. He had a job to do.

As Fergus cleaned his nails with the brush in the scrub room, he averted his eyes from the container where Ailee's kidney waited to be transplanted.

When Fergus and Dr Harry entered the theatre, William lay anaesthetised, his abdomen exposed. The scrub sister handed Fergus the bowl and sponge forceps so he could prep.

Fergus drew a deep breath. Renowned for his perfectionism, this would be his most meticulous transplant yet.

'Now, that's a beautiful kidney,' Dr Harry said nonchalantly.

'It's the most beautiful kidney in the world,' Fergus stated, and then he cleared his mind of the external distractions and set about placing Ailee's kidney in William's pelvis.

The donor kidney was seated near William's bladder so that the ureter could be easily connected through an incision in the lower part of his body. William's old kidneys would not be removed.

When Ailee surfaced slowly through the anaesthetic mist, she realised she had returned to her bed on the ward. Gingerly she turned her head and it seemed there were bright splotches around every wall. That was funny—she hadn't noticed those that morning.

The next time she woke up she realised the splotches were arrangements of flowers—baskets and baskets of orchids and bougainvillea. She didn't need anyone to tell her who they were from.

Her throat hurt and she ran her roughened tongue over dry lips.

'Have some ice,' a deep voice said, and she opened her mouth for the chip of ice without worrying why Fergus was there. She smiled dreamily. Of course he was.

The ice melted away the fur on her tongue and she savoured the feeling as moisture disintegrated the dryness.

The intravenous lines in her arm caught on the sheet

and a large hand came across and gently disentangled them for her. She turned her head slowly and Fergus sat in the chair beside her bed. 'Hello, sleepyhead. How is your pain?'

'Not too bad if I don't move,' she croaked, and he slid the controls of her patient controlled analgesia into her hand.

'You have to move a bit. Don't forget your "dope-on-a-rope". Press your button for the patient analgesia when you have pain. It works quickly and it won't let you overdose.'

'Yes, Doctor.' She was too tired to fight against how good it was to see him.

'Cheeky already.'

'Mmm-hmmm,' she murmured, and fell asleep again.

The next time she woke up her mother was sitting on the chair and she wondered if she'd dreamed that Fergus had been there.

Her mother offered her some ice. 'How are you, darling?'

'Fine, Mum.' She shifted her head and the pain in her flank reminded her to be careful. She felt the control in her hand and gave herself a click of pain relief. She had to move. When the pain receded she sighed and smiled at her mother. 'How's William?'

'He's doing well up in High Dependency. His new kidney is working already.'

'That's great.' She stretched out her arm gingerly and she couldn't believe how that simple movement could set off so many pain receptors in her side. Her mother picked up the cup of ice and handed it to her and she took another piece. Heavenly.

Three days after Ailee and William's operations, Fergus could wait no longer.

'Sophie, we need to talk.'

Fergus hoped she was ready to talk about Ailee now without becoming upset.

His daughter had been avoiding him and every time he broached the subject she drifted away, but he was wearing her down. He ached for her pain but he hoped she knew he hadn't deliberately set out to hurt her.

'I'm listening.' Sophie didn't meet his eyes but at least she'd sat down this time.

Fergus sat next to her and took her hand in his. 'I'm sorry I hurt you with my friendship with Ailee, but three days ago Ailee had her operation and she's getting better now.' He let the words sink in. Fergus watched his daughter, and to his relief she didn't pull away or run screaming from the room.

'The thing is, sweetheart, I've grown to love Ailee and I want to include her in our lives.'

Sophie sighed. 'I know, Dad. I guess I saw it the first day. I even think I could love Ailee, too. And I'm sorry I said all those things about hating you both, but it is pretty scary thinking that what happened to Mummy could happen to Ailee. I don't ever want to be that sad again.'

Fergus squeezed her hand. 'Neither do I, baby. But I think we could be really happy with Ailee in our lives.'

Sophie sighed heavily. 'Well, she's had the operation now.'

Fergus caught his daughter's chin gently and looked into the eyes so similar to his own. 'And who was the person who told me we all have to take risks if something is important enough?'

Sophie sighed again. 'Me.'

He slipped his arm around her shoulders and hugged her. 'I love you, Sophie, and I always will. And we will be a family, hopefully with Ailee as a part of it.' He wondered how far he could stretch their new friendship. 'I'm going in to visit her today—would you like to come?'

To his relief Sophie nodded.

Ailee looked up and smiled when she saw Fergus, and her eyes widened when she saw who was standing beside him at the door.

Sophie came in slowly and looked reassured to see Ailee sitting up in a chair beside the bed. 'Can I speak to Ailee on her own, Dad?'

Fergus looked across and raised his eyebrows. 'I guess so, if it's OK with Ailee.'

Ailee nodded. 'Sure.'

'How are you?' Sophie crept close but was careful not to bump the chair.

Ailee patted the seat next to her and waited while Sophie sat down. 'I'm getting better every day.'

Sophie chewed her lip. 'How come you weren't scared to give away your kidney?'

'You didn't see me on the morning of the operation.' Ailee spread her hands to measure the size. 'I had butterflies bigger than bats in my tummy.'

'Yes.' Sophie smiled at the thought. 'But how come you still gave it away?'

Ailee tilted her head. 'I think what you are asking is why I did something you think is a little dangerous when I didn't have to—is that right?'

Sophie nodded.

'When my brother first became unwell, my mother thought just like you. She didn't want to risk me getting sick, too, and she was frightened something would go wrong.'

Ailee tilted her head. 'Say I didn't give my kidney to my brother. Imagine if William became really sick and died and I never got sick and lived to be an old lady with two kidneys.'

She looked into Sophie's eyes. 'I think I'd be pretty sad and selfish at the end. I'd know I hadn't dared to give up something I didn't need just in case something went wrong, when I could have easily saved my brother's life.'

Sophie raised her eyebrows not unlike her father's. 'I don't think it was easy, what you did.'

Ailee smiled. 'Maybe not, but I have spent a lot of time around sick people, especially those with end-stage kidney disease, and they have a tough life with a lot of things taken away from them. From where they are sitting, I bet what I did looks easy.'

Sophie nodded, semi-converted but not convinced. 'What if you get kidney disease later in life and need a kidney?'

'The chance of that is smaller than a lot of things. What if I got run over by a bus or travelled to another country and had an accident?' Ailee gave a tiny shrug.

'Should I stay home safely just in case? Should you not go skiing because it's dangerous and certainly not go to New Zealand because it's a long way from home?'

'I'm sorry I got scared,' Sophie said in a small voice. Ailee held open her arms and Sophie crept closer to lean gently against her.

'I'm sorry I scared you. But it was very nice of you to care what happened to me.' She stroked Sophie's hair. 'Do you want to know a secret?'

Sophie nodded and Ailee went on in a whisper, 'There was one thing I was scared of. I wouldn't let myself fall in love with your father in case something went wrong.'

Sophie leant back so she could see Ailee's face. 'And now that you are getting better?'

Ailee raised her eyes to the man standing at the door, trying not to listen. 'As soon as I'm well, I'm going to chase him as hard as I can.'

'OK,' Sophie whispered back.

Ailee looked up and her mother was standing beside Fergus at the door.

'Hi, Mum, come in.' Ailee smiled at Sophie.

Helen and Fergus came to stand beside the chairs.

'This is Sophie, Fergus's daughter. Sophie, my mum.'

Helen smiled. 'Hello, Sophie. It's lovely to meet you.' Helen raised her eyebrows at her daughter, as if to say, *Why didn't you tell me?*

Ailee mouthed, 'Later'. Her mother smiled. Helen looked at Sophie. 'Would you like to come and meet Ailee's brother, William?'

Sophie nodded and stood up. She smiled at Ailee. 'Ailee wants to talk to Dad anyway.'

'Does she, now?' said Helen, and both were grinning conspiratorially as they left.

Fergus sat down beside her and took her hand in his. 'That didn't seem to go too badly from where I was standing.'

'How did you convince Sophie to visit?'

He shrugged ruefully. 'She seemed ready. I found her looking up live donor web sites on the internet yesterday. I think she'll be fine. I know she'll be happier when you're safely home. As will I!'

Ailee smiled and squeezed the larger hand in hers. 'I understand.'

He looked at her and smiled. 'I don't think you do.'

'I think Sophie is very brave and wonderful, like her father.'

'I haven't started to be brave yet,' he said cryptically. 'Now, how are you today?'

She looked down at their entwined fingers and savoured the feeling. Fergus had been a little more open with his affection every day since her operation, and she was happy to let it all progress slowly while she recuperated. The warmth of expectation had been growing since that first morning when he had been there when she'd woken up.

'Better every day.'

'Keep going. How about you come home to my house to recuperate instead of your mother's?'

Ailee's brow creased. 'Are you going to take up nursing, Mr McVicker?'

'Only one patient. And I was thinking full-time care. For ever.'

Ailee looked up at the serious tone of his voice.

He shook his head because she still didn't get it. 'Do you realise how much I love you and have loved you since the first time I saw you?'

She shook her head, but she was beginning to realise. Especially with the way he was looking at her now. 'I knew you fancied me,' she teased.

'That, too, but I was thinking "ever after" when you woke beside me on the plane that first morning.'

Ailee's eyes widened. 'That's not true.'

His lips twitched. 'I'm afraid so. Why do you think I was so mean to you when you arrived on the ward? You broke my heart when you left me in Singapore.'

She looked him up and down. 'You look pretty hale and hearty for someone with a broken heart.'

He squeezed her hand back. 'I know you won't get away this time. I can relax.'

Despite the banter, she realised he'd given up on waiting and she couldn't ask him to wait any longer. He'd been patient enough.

He smiled at her crookedly and Ailee felt the tears prickle her eyes.

'I want to do this properly. I should wait for you to be strong and be somewhere romantic.' He glanced at the floor. 'Would you like me to kneel?'

Ailee bit her lip and swallowed the lump in her throat. 'Absolutely not.'

Fergus smiled and dropped to one knee beside the chair. 'Tough.'

'Darling Ailee.' He took her hand. 'Would you do me the very great honour of becoming my wife?'

Ailee reached across, careful of her wound, and kissed his lips.

'I would be privileged, Fergus. Thank you. Now, get up quickly before someone sees you.' She glanced furtively at the empty doorway.

Fergus was smiling openly now. 'No. I think I'll ring the nurse's call button and get Rita in here to see what you've brought me to.'

Ailee tugged on his hand. 'Fergus. Get up. And don't make me laugh. It hurts.'

He climbed to his feet and slipped an arm gently around her shoulders before kissing her. 'The last thing I want to do is hurt you. In fact, I'm going to spend the next fifty years looking after you.'

Ailee smiled unsteadily at the man she loved with all her heart. 'And I'll look after you, my love.'

They held a makeshift engagement party on the ward, and Sophie pushed William around in his wheelchair.

'That was quick,' was all she said. 'I've always wanted a brother.'

CHAPTER TWELVE

THE wedding was held in the gardens of Fergus's home with red lanterns strewn among the trees.

The exotic mix of Singapore orchids and splashes of vivid colour from branches of bougainvillea highlighted the red cheongsam worn by the young bridesmaid as she arrived. The Wedding March began.

Head high and smiling, Sophie slowly walked down the carpet across the grass that led to the roofless chapel Fergus had created for his bride.

For the last month he'd watched his daughter and Ailee do all the feminine things Sophie should have been doing for the last few years.

Clothes shopping and more clothes shopping. Hairdresser visits and dancing lessons, so Sophie and William could dance with the bride and groom at the reception.

Redecorating her own room and interfering in the refurbishment of what would now be Fergus and Ailee's room.

Fergus watched with pride as his daughter swayed

sedately up the aisle and took her place beside him as they waited for the bride.

'You look beautiful,' Fergus said, as Sophie arrived.

'Wait until you see Ailee,' Sophie whispered, and the gasp from those assembled heralded the bride's arrival.

Fergus watched his bride-to-be enter and his heart rate quickened as the music swelled. He had waited for this day for three months.

Accompanied by a new and vibrant William, Ailee smiled at him from the end of the carpet.

She'd chosen to dress simply in a pure white, high-collared sheath, which accentuated her height and slimness, and a tiny veil that Fergus ached to lift.

When Ailee stopped at the flower-strewn altar, William transferred her hand from his arm to Fergus's.

She looked at her husband-to-be and exhilaration expanded in Fergus's chest. He wanted to sweep her up in his arms and spin her around.

Finally this moment had arrived and he couldn't help but look at the minister to get on with it.

'Dearly beloved…' The minister hurried into speech and Fergus held Ailee's gaze as the words washed over them. 'I love you,' he whispered, and squeezed her hand.

'I love you, too,' she said, and he could see the shine of happy tears in her eyes. He loved her so much he hoped he could speak the vows through the tightness in his throat.

But when the time came, both their promises carried clearly across the garden. Fergus gazed into Ailee's eyes, hoping she knew how proud he was at this moment to stand beside her.

When the service was complete, Fergus lifted the tiny veil and her face was there before him. They smiled at each other and then he bent and rested his lips against hers to taste the sweetness to come. He kissed his bride, finally sure that everything would turn out right.

Ailee and Fergus turned to the congregation and Fergus tucked his wife's hand firmly into his arm, leaving no one in any doubt that he meant to keep Ailee close by his side.

The minister's voice boomed. 'It is my pleasure to introduce Mr Fergus and Mrs Ailee McVicker.' The applause washed over the happy couple as they walked back up the carpet.

Guests milled and spilled out into the garden and the sun shone down on everyone. Ailee's mother sniffed happily into a handkerchief lent to her by Dr Harry's wife.

William and Sophie came up to congratulate them and there was a twinkle of mischief in Ailee's brother's eyes.

'Hey, bro,' he said, with a smile to Fergus. 'I'll take great care of her kidney if you take good care of the rest of her.'

Fergus laughed. 'I'll spend my life doing that,' he said, as he smiled across at the woman he loved.

Can you tell from first impressions whether someone could become your closest friend?

Lydia, Jacqueline, Carol and Alix are four very different women, each facing their own problems in life. When they are thrown together by the hands of fate, none of them could ever guess how close they would become or where their friendship would lead them.

A heartfelt, emotional tale of friendship and problems shared from a multi-million copy bestselling author.

On sale 18th August 2006

FREE!

4 Books
and a surprise gift!

We would like to take this opportunity to thank you for reading this Mills & Boon® book by offering you the chance to take FOUR more specially selected titles from the Medical Romance™ series absolutely FREE! We're also making this offer to introduce you to the benefits of the Mills & Boon® Reader Service™—

- ★ FREE home delivery
- ★ FREE gifts and competitions
- ★ FREE monthly Newsletter
- ★ Exclusive Reader Service offers
- ★ Books available before they're in the shops

Accepting these FREE books and gift places you under no obligation to buy, you may cancel at any time, even after receiving your free shipment. Simply complete your details below and return the entire page to the address below. You don't even need a stamp!

YES! Please send me 4 free Medical Romance books and a surprise gift. I understand that unless you hear from me, I will receive 6 superb new titles every month for just £2.80 each, postage and packing free. I am under no obligation to purchase any books and may cancel my subscription at any time. The free books and gift will be mine to keep in any case.

M6ZEF

Ms/Mrs/Miss/Mr ....Initials...............................

BLOCK CAPITALS PLEASE

Surname ....

Address..

....

....Postcode ....

Send this whole page to:
UK: FREEPOST CN81, Croydon, CR9 3WZ